Spare Change

Spare Change

By
Aubrey Mace

Bonneville Books
Springville, Utah

The views expressed within this work are the sole responsibility of the author and do not necessarily reflect the position of Cedar Fort, Inc., or any other entity.

This is a work of fiction. The characters, names, incidents, places, and dialogue are products of the author's imagination, and are not to be construed as real.

ISBN 13: 978-1-59955-150-0

Published by Bonneville Books, an imprint of Cedar Fort, Inc., 2373 W. 700 S., Springville, UT 84663
Distributed by Cedar Fort, Inc., www.cedarfort.com

LIBRARY OF CONGRESS CATALOGING-IN-PUBLICATION DATA
    Mace, Aubrey.
      Spare change / Aubrey Mace.
        p. cm.
      ISBN 978-1-59955-150-0 (acid-free paper)
      1. Young women—Fiction. 2. Domestic fiction. I. Title.
      PS3613.A2717S63 2008
      813'.6—dc22
                                    2008000480

Cover design by Nicole Williams
Cover design © 2008 by Lyle Mortimer
Edited and typeset by Kimiko M. Hammari

Printed in the United States of America

10 9 8 7 6 5 4 3 2 1

Printed on acid-free paper

acknowledgments

I would like to thank Cedar Fort and especially Kammi and Kimiko for making this experience one I will never forget. I will be forever grateful to you for taking a chance on me.

I also want to mention all of the wonderful doctors and nurses (and secretaries) I have worked with over the years. Thank you for your friendship and for understanding why I'd rather answer the phone than stick needles into people.

To Dawna and Glen Bradford, for living lives worthy of emulation. Grandpa, thanks for the adventures. Grandma, thank you for not minding the holes in the driveway, and for your time.

And last, many thanks to anyone who ever made the effort to read something I wrote. It is because of you that this book is a reality.

To the best family and friends a girl could have, for your love and support. I wish I could name every one of you, but it would take pages. You know who you are. You picked me up and dusted me off and told me to keep trying, and I never would have made it this far without your kind words and encouragement.

And for Rusty Eyre, who lost his battle with cancer.
We miss you.

chapter 1

Since its beginning, the U.S. Mint has produced over 288.7 billion pennies. Lined up edge to edge, these pennies would circle the earth 137 times.

—Americans for Common Cents (www.pennies.org)

I f you've ever gotten to the drive-thru window or the front of the line at the grocery store only to discover that you're short on cash, you know what I mean when I say that everyone hates pennies. Of course, most of the penny counting has been reduced by the fact that everything is now credit-based in the United States. Hardly anyone carries cash anymore. It is not an uncommon sight to see someone flip out their Visa to cover their Super Big Gulp. I'm ashamed to admit I've done it myself. Those who do pay with cash quite often tell the clerk to keep the pennies. The look on a customer's face when you attempt to hand them their one penny is priceless—like you're trying to get away with something devious and they know it. Even if you do persuade them to accept the offending article, that's no guarantee that they will make it further than the door. Lately it seems that in every parking lot, somewhere between the car and the entrance to wherever I'm going, I find change on the ground. Between inflation and our short attention spans, pennies don't stand a chance. People don't want to be bothered with carrying around worthless coins.

My name is Riley Madsen, and I'm going to do something with all those tiny pennies that everyone loathes, starting today, January 1, with my New Year's resolution.

I hate New Year's resolutions. In fact, I think that New Year's resolutions are part of the reason January and February are two of the most depressing months of the year. Winter is at the point where it seems that it will never end, and already you've botched all your good intentions. It's enough to make anyone feel down. So this year, I was ready to flout tradition and forget about the resolutions altogether. But when I went home last night for New Year's Eve, someone had other plans for me.

I sat in the living room with my sisters and little brother, listening to Dick Clark blare in the background. It was 11:00 PM, and my family was making their traditional New Year's resolutions. My mother passed around sheets of paper and pencils so that everyone could record their shortcomings and how they planned to improve over the coming year. I watched as my five-year-old brother, Mitch, drew a picture of himself holding an ice cream cone bigger than he was.

"You'd better get busy with your resolutions, Mitch," I said.

"I am," Mitch replied.

"But that's just a picture of you with an enormous ice cream cone."

"I know."

"I don't get it. What's your resolution?"

"Eat more ice cream," he said seriously. He had a death grip on his pencil, coloring in the cone so fiercely that I feared destruction of the page and perhaps the table underneath was imminent.

My mother wiped her hands on a dish towel as she emerged from the kitchen.

"Mitch, honey, remember we talked about some good resolutions for you to choose?" She rolled her eyes and mouthed to me over his head, "He just doesn't get it."

I tried not to chuckle, pursing my lips together tightly.

"I decided to choose my own. I like ice cream, and there are lots of kinds I haven't tried yet."

"Funny, but it sounds quite logical when he explains his reasoning. Maybe that should be my resolution too," I said, cocking my head to one side thoughtfully. I got up and followed my mother back into the kitchen with my empty page. I hoisted myself up to sit on the counter near the sink where she was rinsing dishes.

"What does your list look like, Riley?" she said, stacking the plates neatly in the dishwasher.

I held the blank paper over my head where I hoped she couldn't reach, but she was too quick for me and grabbed it from my hands.

"Where are your resolutions, honey? It's almost midnight."

"I'm twenty-three, Mom. I'm too old for this."

"Well, you're never too old to try to improve yourself, until you're dead."

I sighed loudly. "I'm just tired of choosing the same things every year and never doing any of them. At least if I don't make any resolutions in the first place, I won't be disappointed when I don't follow through." I knew my mother was making mental notes of all the flaws in this logic, but I persisted. "I mean, how many times can you not lose the same ten pounds?"

"Oh, I don't know. I do it every year." Her eyes twinkled with amusement as she closed the dishwasher and pressed the start button.

I felt terrible. Here I was on New Year's Eve trying to convince my mother that resolutions were just another way to set yourself up for failure. Even my little brother had his priorities straight. What was wrong with me? All I had to look forward to was another year with no real prospects, another year with no one to kiss at midnight.

"If you don't like the way you've dealt with the new year in the past, do it differently this year," Mom said. "A whole list of resolutions can be daunting. Pick just one thing that you want to do; it can even be something really easy. Once you find out you can accomplish it, you might be ready to move on to bigger things next year."

When I didn't say anything, she started tickling my arm like she did when I was a little girl.

"Riley, you're still young. I hate for you to be so cynical. You have the capacity to do so much good, if you'd only let yourself. You don't have to move a mountain to make a difference."

I didn't know what to say. At that moment, I felt selfish and mean, and all I wanted to do was go home to bed and pretend it wasn't New Year's Eve at all.

"I know you'll come up with something," she said finally, kissing the top of my head and walking back to the living room.

I sat on the counter, thinking about what my mother said. I couldn't help feeling that I was being singled out for unnecessary torture. What was the absolute smallest change I could make at the least possible inconvenience to myself?

Change, change . . . change? I reached into the pocket of my jeans and pulled out a handful of coins, mostly pennies. This was perfect. At the end of every day, I would save all my pennies in a jar. Then, at the end of the year, I could do something nice for myself!

I deposited the coins back into my pocket and quickly scrawled my resolution onto the paper I'd been dragging around all night. I waltzed smugly back into the family room to join the others. I had beaten the system. Emily, Olivia, and Charlotte were playing Monopoly, waiting for the ball to drop. My youngest sister, Katie, had found my purse and was trying out my lipstick, Sassy Pink, from her nose to her chin. Mitch's stack of ice-cream-related artwork was growing. And my dad was asleep in the recliner, snoring rhythmically.

Happy New Year.

chapter 2

All the world's a stage, and all the men and women merely players. They have their exits and their entrances; And one man in his time plays many parts.

—William Shakespeare, *As You Like It*

I have never been accused of being a morning person. Still, as I drove to work on January 2, it was hard to wipe the smug smile from my face. I felt like I had a huge secret from the rest of the world—an agenda. It was going to be so much fun deciding what to do with the money at the end of the year. There were plenty of options, and I amused myself by pondering the possibilities.

It might be fun to take a little vacation. Of course, it would have to be a very little vacation, but I might have enough for gas money, or maybe a plane ticket. I've always wanted to take a train somewhere. Or I could buy some clothes. Everyone is looking for a change at the beginning of a new year. I've always wanted a pair of leather boots. I wonder how much money I will have by the end of the year. Assuming that I put in ten pennies a day . . . I almost always end up with change every day, but not all of it is pennies. So, ten cents a day for a year is . . . $36.50.

Well, so much for the travel plans. Even if it was thirty cents a day, I'd barely break a hundred dollars. The excited feeling I woke up with deflated as quickly as if it were a balloon popped with a needle. I decided I'd better start thinking of a reward on a smaller scale.

I parked my car at the back of the lot under a row of trees where I always did. The bad thing about getting there early was that the lot wasn't always plowed, but since it didn't snow the previous night, I managed to get into the building without too much trouble. I'm not much of a snow person, and I hate being cold. This morning, I had on a heavy brown coat, a scarf, and gloves, and I was still freezing.

I work in a hospital. Well, to be more accurate, I work near a hospital, in a clinic where we treat cancer patients. Whenever I tell people where I work, their first question is almost unanimously the same.

"Are you a nurse?"

This gets really old after a while, since I am not a nurse. When I tell them politely that I am a secretary, the response I get is usually one of two things. If it is a tactful person, they usually reply with something to the effect of how they don't blame me and they could never be a nurse either. The more common response generally goes like this: "Well, someone has to answer the phone, right?"

Like they're rocket scientists, but understand the fundamental need for people to serve in brainless positions like mine. I actually had someone give me this response once: "Oh. So, when are you going back to school?"

I sometimes feel like how the canaries must have felt, being sent into the mine to make sure it was safe before the really important people decided to show up.

Expendable, that's me. But it's okay. I understand that it takes a certain kind of person to be a nurse, and at the end of the day, I'd rather be the person answering the phone than the person sticking needles into people.

I opened the door to the office and took a seat at my computer. I logged on and quickly skimmed over my emails, one of which was an invitation to join the hospital's annual weight-loss/healthy lifestyle program for the new year. Not *this* year. I gleefully hit the delete button.

Kate came in and sat down, lost in a patient's chart. Kate is one of the nurses I work with, and one of the most beautiful people I have ever seen who isn't a celebrity. She has naturally curly blonde hair and eyes the color of grass in the summertime. Most of the time, I feel like a grub sitting next to her.

I wish my hair were curly, but it's completely stick straight, despite any of my efforts to the contrary. I tried to get a perm once, but the curl disappeared after only a few days. The stylist said that almost never happens. Trust me to be the exception. My hair is also the most boring shade of brown. My best friend, Lauren, tried to dye it blonde at her house when we were about fifteen. I found some hair dye on clearance at the grocery store; it was one of the only truly wild, impulsive things I've ever done. Apparently, there was a reason it was on sale. While green is a lovely shade for eyes, it is rather frightening for hair. I've learned to stop messing with it, as any efforts to make drastic changes only seem to anger it.

"Riley, I didn't hear you sneak in." Kate was alternating between charting and munching on a piece of dry toast and a bowl of cottage cheese.

"Nice breakfast," I commented. I pulled an oversized chocolate chip muffin out of my bag and set it on the counter in front of me with exaggerated flair.

Kate noticed it immediately and groaned. "Where did you get that?" she asked, unable to tear her eyes away.

"At the gas station. It's where all the really cool people buy their breakfast. What's up with the Starvation Special you've got going over there?"

She poked savagely at the cottage cheese with her plastic spoon.

"The diet starts today." She looked back at my muffin and sighed.

I turned so that I was fully facing her. "Kate, I want you to listen to me. New Year's resolutions are a scam, a ploy to make us feel bad about ourselves. Look at me—I've given up resolutions, and I feel great."

"You didn't make any resolutions this year?" she asked skeptically.

"Well, I did make one, but only because my mother forced me to. And it's so easy it shouldn't even qualify."

"What is it?"

"I can't tell you; it's too silly. Do you want half of my muffin?"

Kate looked at it longingly, but her steel will kicked in.

"No, I'm okay." She spooned some of the cottage cheese onto the corner of her toast and bit it off without much enthusiasm.

I shook my head sadly. "You'll see I'm right. After about two weeks, you'll be begging to come to the dark side, and we'll be here waiting," I said, patting the muffin wrapper. As I was about to tear into the muffin, the phone rang.

"Landmark Cancer Treatment Center. This is Riley."

"Well, you're never going to believe what happened to me last night," Lauren said, her voice heavy with sarcasm.

"Happy New Year to you too, sunshine."

"So, I'm driving home from this party at about 1:45, and my cell phone starts ringing. And I'm thinking, who would call me this late? There must be some sort of emergency or something. I've got one eye on the road and I'm fumbling through my purse trying to find my phone, but when I finally got to it, I accidentally dropped it on the floor. I'm really worried about who it could be, so I'm leaning over trying to reach it, and suddenly there's blue and red lights flashing in my rearview mirror."

"Oh, Lauren! Why didn't you just pull over to find your phone? You could have rolled the car."

"It wasn't a problem," she said, brushing it off. "I had everything under control."

"Then why did you get pulled over?"

She exhaled with exaggerated irritation. "The officer said I was weaving back and forth, which I'm sure I wasn't. I'm a really good driver," she protested.

"So, then what happened?" I asked eagerly. Luckily, none of my other lines were ringing. One of the most frustrating things about my job is having to put someone on hold in the middle of their story.

"Well, Stewart . . ."

"Stewart? Who's Stewart?"

"The officer who pulled me over."

"Oh, so you're on a first name basis now, are you?"

"Hardly. Anyway, *Officer* Stewart asked me why I was swerving all over the road, and I told him I wasn't, and he asked me how much I had to drink. I told him that I don't drink, and he started in on me about how everyone gives him the same story, and why can't people just admit when they've made a mistake instead of trying to cover it up. I told him the only mistake I made was dropping my phone into the depths of my purse where I'd never find it if I needed it, but he didn't believe me. So he made me get out of the car and walk a straight line, which I did, but he still wasn't satisfied. He even made me take a breathalyzer test! It was so humiliating!"

"Was he embarrassed when he found out you were telling the truth?" I asked, unable to stifle a giggle.

"Not exactly. He apologized for thinking that I was drunk but proceeded to give me a lecture about how playing with your cell phone while you're driving is just as dangerous as drinking. I still got a ticket for impaired driving," she said grumpily.

"I hate to say it, but . . ."

"Don't tell me you're taking his side!" Lauren said furiously.

"He was just doing his job."

"That's not how this was supposed to go. I tell you about my terrible night, and you feel sorry for me and sympathize. Whatever happened to innocent until proven guilty?"

"Of course I feel sorry for you. But you have to admit, he does have a point. And you can't blame him for being suspicious. New Year's Eve is the biggest drunk driving day of the year."

"I suppose. It was actually kind of funny. Toward the end, he seemed really self-conscious all of the sudden. It was like he could barely look at me. I almost felt sorry for him."

"He probably thought you were cute and felt bad about hassling you."

"He did say that citing beautiful women was the worst part of his job," she said grudgingly.

"Lauren! Already your night was better than mine, even with the ticket. Was he cute?"

"Very," she sighed.

"Maybe if you start driving crazy on a regular basis, you'll run into him again."

"There's no need. He told me I should sign up for a driving class, and if I complete it and pay the ticket, it won't go on my record."

"I don't understand. Unless he's . . ."

". . . teaching the class," she said smugly.

"You are shameless. I should go, but I definitely want to hear more about this later."

"There's nothing to tell—it's just a silly fantasy. He probably has a wife and three kids. And a dog."

"Yeah, that's why he practically asked you out."

"Traffic school doesn't count."

"By the way, who was calling you in the middle of the night on your cell phone?" I asked curiously.

"That's the funniest part. I'd completely forgotten about it until I got home, and I didn't recognize the number, but he did leave a message."

"He?"

"Yeah, it was some guy with a slurry voice, whispering about how it must have been fate that we met, and how much he enjoyed our spontaneous dip in the swimming pool at midnight."

"You must have been at the top of your game! First the Pool Guy, then Stewart . . . how many other hearts did you break before the night was through?"

"Oh, please. He obviously had the wrong number."

"How can you be sure?"

"Aside from the fact that I didn't ring in the New Year in the pool, he also said he loved my pink hair."

"Well, either Pool Girl was slightly less enchanted with their encounter than Pool Guy, or she was too drunk to remember her phone number." One of my other lines started ringing. "Now I really have to go. We'll discuss Stewart versus Pool Guy later."

"I'll start making the list of pros and cons."

By the time I hung up, three lines were ringing, and I didn't have any more time to devote to considering Lauren's new possible conquest. Before I knew it, I was buried in the business of the day.

. . . .

"Riley, do you have time to go pick up the chemo?" Sarah asked. Sarah is another nurse I work with, probably the one I am closest to. She is incredibly short—about five-foot-one—and she has a hilarious personality. She throws out one-liners like she was reading them from a script. I had started working at the Landmark Hospital Cancer Treatment Center over a year ago, and I felt lucky to have lots of acquaintances. But whenever I went to the hospital with Sarah, she was greeted by nearly everyone we passed. It seemed that Sarah was everyone's friend—a quality I both envied and admired.

"Sure." I walked back into one of the rooms and got a mauve puke bucket labeled CHEMO in angry black letters. I pulled on a pair of blue latex gloves and headed down the hall.

"Anything else?" I called out behind me, already halfway out the door.

Sarah's head popped around the corner. "Yeah. Stop and check the ice cream flavors at the snack bar."

"Seriously, you guys are killing me," I heard Kate's voice say before the door closed behind me.

. . . .

On my second day at the hospital, one of the nurses had sent me to the pharmacy to pick up the chemo with the same strange request—stop and check the ice cream flavors. I never ate much ice cream before I started there, except birthdays and the occasional pint of Ben & Jerry's. But these were hardcore ice cream women, and after a couple of months, I was hooked.

So, as I carried my chemo bucket that first time, clutched tightly in my latex-gloved hands, I was a little apprehensive about doing everything just right. I knocked on the pharmacy door and waited for what seemed like an eternity before someone let me in.

"Hi, I'm Riley. I'm here to pick up the chemo. Is it ready?"

"Almost. He's mixing it now. You must be new. Do you want to watch?"

I nodded and followed the elderly volunteer in the pink jacket to an open door leading into a much smaller room. Inside, a man stood covered in so many layers of gowns and shields that it appeared he was expecting either a disease outbreak or a nuclear holocaust. His gloved hands disappeared through holes in a glass case, mixing and measuring the necessary evils. He looked just like a mad scientist. I realized that I was holding my breath, not wanting to breathe in any toxic fumes that might be dancing around the tiny space.

"I'll be done in a minute, okay?" was the muffled comment from the pharmacist, breaking the heavy silence.

I walked back to the main door, feeling relieved to be farther away from the chemo room. After a while, he reappeared carrying several harmless looking bags of IV fluid and a syringe of something red that looked positively lethal. He put these into separate Ziploc bags, all of which stated CHEMOTHERAPY—TOXIC, before depositing them into a heap in my bucket.

"Thanks," I said, almost running out the door into the halls of the hospital. All I wanted to do was get back to the office and get rid of the chemo, but I promised my new coworkers that I would check on the ice cream situation. I poked my head into the snack bar and squinted at the whiteboard. Ice cream flavors were labeled in alternating cheerful colors. Vanilla, cookie dough, raspberry sherbet, and butter pecan.

On the way back, I repeated the flavors to myself over and over under my breath.

"Vanilla, cookie dough, raspberry sherbet, butter pecan."

I was sort of glad to be wearing a badge in case someone mistook me for an escapee from the psych ward and tried to return me. All the time, my stomach churned, and I felt more and more like the poison I was carrying in the bucket was somehow seeping through the gloves and into my skin.

"Vanilla, cookie dough, raspberry sherbet, butter pecan."

I sped down the hall, rounding the corner toward the office and staring straight ahead. I noticed that I was breathing faster and told myself not to think about what was in the bucket. *It's all in your mind; you're perfectly safe.*

"Vanilla, cookie dough, raspberry sherbet, butter pecan."

The door made its customary ring, announcing that I had returned. I practically threw the chemo bucket at Sarah, tearing off the gloves and feeling an overwhelming sense of irrational relief.

"What kinds of ice cream do they have today?" Sarah said eagerly.

I rattled off my list in a monotone voice I barely recognized as my own.

"Moose Tracks! I wanted Moose Tracks," she pouted. "Oh well, there's always tomorrow." She took the bucket and went merrily on her way to hook someone up to the poison.

Personally, I fancied butter pecan, but it didn't really matter. I wasn't very hungry anymore.

. . . .

Today the flavors were chocolate chip, rocky road, strawberry cheesecake, and mango sorbet. I dropped off the chemo at the office, picked up everyone's ice cream, and wolfed down a double scoop of Rocky Road. It's amazing what you can get used to. I put my change, four pennies, into the pocket of my scrubs.

chapter 3

We must be willing to let go of the life we have planned,
so as to have the life that is waiting for us.

—E. M. Forster

B y the time the first day of February rolled around, I was
the proud owner of 158 pennies, which hardly seemed an
auspicious beginning. Still, the lifespan of this resolution
was already an improvement on any of its predecessors. At night
after work, I emptied my pockets and put the meager offering into
a large glass jar. No matter how many pennies I added, it seemed
that the jar would never be filled.

I had some slightly more realistic plans now as to what would be
done with my savings, but they were still rather vague and changed
from day to day. Currently I was vacillating between subscribing to
a couple of magazines or going to the bookstore and buying as many
books as I could afford. Since I lived alone, my mailbox was often
empty, and there was nothing quite as exciting as finding something
in there that didn't require payment. It's that pleasant thrill that
comes with forgetting something is coming until it arrives unexpectedly. But then, I can't remember the last time I went to the bookstore
and bought whatever I wanted. I just couldn't help feeling that there
must be something more meaningful. Something . . . bigger.

Anyway, I had plenty of time to figure it out. At the moment,
I had bigger things to consider. I had a date—with an actual guy.
A blind date, to be specific; Lauren was setting me up.

Again.

I love Lauren, like a sister. I just wish she'd stop trying to pawn me off on every available guy she meets. Lauren is what she calls "happily single." She says it's the "happily" part that makes the difference. She is perfectly content to live her own life until Mr. Right just magically drops into her lap someday. I've tried to explain to her that it doesn't work that way. You know—you have to kiss a lot of frogs to find your handsome prince. But she believes in fate. Stop wearing yourself out running in circles and kissing frogs, and wait for the prince to find you.

Which is why she sets me up on endless blind dates, while she sits comfortably on her couch on Friday night, eating cookie dough straight from the tube and watching back-to-back episodes of *Cold Case Files* on cable. I envy her coolness, her Zen-like detachment about the whole thing. Still, I find it odd that she seems to have this untiring need to see me settled. How could she be so engaged in my future and so nonchalant about her own?

James is the guy I'm supposed to go out with this time. Apparently, he is twenty-six, never married, tall, and enjoys mountain biking, soccer, and football. He works in a store selling—you guessed it—sporting goods. Already, he sounds too athletic for me. I am a complete dork where sports are concerned. I'm told my parents met in high school on the tennis team, but it appears that sometimes hand-eye coordination skips a generation. I suppose a mountain bike expedition is within the realm of possibility, but anything beyond that is getting iffy.

I once had a rather tragic blind date experience that involved bowling. I ended up going with the guy (another Lauren pick) and all his friends to the bowling alley. Like a first date isn't stressful enough without throwing athletic ability into the mix. I hadn't been bowling since I was five, and it didn't take long to remember why. The first ball I threw was a strike, and there was me, thinking that I finally found something semi-sporty I was good at.

You've heard of beginner's luck? The rest of my turns were a mix of gutter balls and several weak efforts that barely made it to the pins without actually knocking any down. That was our first and last date. I guess good bowling skills were important to him in a successful relationship.

Personally, I'm a big fan of the dinner and a movie combo. You get a chance to talk, find out something about your date at dinner. If it's going terribly, you hide in a dark movie theater where you don't have to speak for the rest of the night, and you can console yourself with a bucket of greasy popcorn. If it's going well, you're sitting very close to a near-stranger in a dark theater, your fingers bumping into his in the popcorn bucket. There's something a little . . . dangerous about the whole thing. At least I would imagine there was, never having actually experienced the second scenario.

Well, I can date anyone once, and it wasn't like my phone was ringing off the hook lately. I just hoped that James didn't want to go skiing.

. . . .

Working in the cancer treatment center is a downer sometimes. On occasion, someone stops by who actually got better, just to say hello. Often, they look so much healthier that it's hard to recognize them. They all seem to exude happiness, a glow around them I imagine has nothing to do with the radiation treatments. But there's a good chance that when someone doesn't show up for their appointment, it isn't because they forgot. There's nothing worse than searching the obituaries and finding a patient.

When I started working there, it unnerved me to see people coming in to begin chemo looking completely healthy, some of them younger than me. Weren't people with cancer supposed to look sick? Ironically, they looked good when they started, but every time they came back for treatments, they looked worse and worse. It was like the environment of the office itself was making them ill. Unfortunately, they often had to travel to the brink of the beyond before they started to improve.

I had a difficult time getting used to it. Seeing all those seemingly vital people depressed me. Before I knew it, my hypochondriac side was out in full force. I couldn't stop thinking about what might be lurking inside me, like a bomb with the timer steadily counting down to zero. Some days, there was a lot of downtime between patients, and I spent most of it thinking about how I could have cancer and not even know it. I fixated on the younger patients especially, studying their movements closely, trying to detect some small outward flaw that would advertise their illness. But there was nothing.

In fact, the only thing that I discovered that they all shared was their attitude. They laughed and joked like there was nothing wrong, and it baffled me. According to the statistics, a large number of these people didn't have much time left. So what did they have to be happy about? Why waste precious energy kidding yourself? Why bother smiling at all?

Maybe it's about making the most of what you have to work with. It took me a while to stop being paranoid, but hanging around death has a way of either making you cling to life or shut down completely. Seeing people face painful treatments and ultimately their own mortality has a way of putting your own bad day into perspective. I try to be nice to all the patients, but some certainly make it easier than others. I watch the nurses, how kind they are, even when I know they are tired or have problems in their own lives.

I often feel superfluous. I'm just waiting for the day when I come to work, only to be informed that they've taken a poll and decided that they could really do without me. Basically, I pull charts, greet the patients, take phone calls, and make appointments. Oh, and pick up everyone's lunch; I seem to do that a lot. Granted, these are all necessary tasks that I perform, but I'm hardly Florence Nightingale. I wish I could do something a little more important.

One of my favorite patients came into the office today— Wallace Hardy. Mr. Hardy has pancreatic cancer, which he recently discovered has spread to his stomach and lungs. He was in remission for a while, but he's back on chemo and radiation now, trying to postpone the inevitable. It took me a few visits to figure out what made me like him so much. One day, I looked at Mr.

Hardy and saw my grandfather. They are similar in appearance: same height (shortish), same slight build, and the same weathered faces with eyes that crinkled when they smiled. They dress the same, in overalls, or plaid shirts and jeans. They have the same dirty fingernails of someone who works with their hands.

Today he was starting a new chemo as the doctors clamored to find something that would slow the deadly onslaught. I gave him a sympathetic smile when he came through the door, but he just brushed it off. I think he prefers to pretend that there is nothing wrong—he's simply coming here to visit. When people did leave with a clean bill of health, if they did, it always broke my heart to see them coming back to start over. And every time I knew there was a better chance that this would be the battle from which they wouldn't return.

I slumped a little lower in my chair and sighed, feeling that this would definitely be an ice cream day. I decided to check my email and was not surprised to find something from Lauren. The subject line said "Operation James—Update." I sipped my Diet Pepsi and opened it a little warily.

> Riley, I gave James your number and told him that he'd better call you. He's pretty busy this weekend—I guess he's running in a marathon somewhere. Can you imagine running 26 miles? I don't think I could run that far even if a bear was chasing me! Anyway, he's really cute. I can't wait for you guys to go out. He could be THE ONE! Call me tonight if you want to go to the laundromat. I have nothing clean left to wear. Love, Lauren.

I clicked the button to reply.

> Dear Hopeless Matchmaker, what are you thinking?! This guy is obviously way too athletic for me, hence the marathon running and other sports-related hobbies. The only thing we probably have in common is carb loading, only I'm not competing in anything; I just like pasta. As I have said on more than one occasion, I'll go out with anybody once, but

I want to go on record as saying that this has disaster written all over it. Will call you tonight when I get home—as much as I would like to spend the evening loafing on the couch, I'm afraid the laundromat is a necessity. P.S. Traffic school is coming up. Have you decided what you're going to wear? :) Love, Riley.

Since it was a pretty slow afternoon, I also went to a couple of discount airfare websites. There were some pretty good deals on roundtrip airfare for under $100 to a few places. If I wanted to, I could pick one at random and use the pennies to fly there just for the day—have an adventure.

Mr. Hardy stopped by my desk on the way out to make his next appointment. He looked pale and tired, but he still smiled when I handed him his reminder card.

"Riley, you're in charge," he called on his way out. This had become something of a joke between us, since I have the least authority of anyone in the office. The first time he said that, it took me off guard because that's what my dad always jokingly told me when he left the house. Mr. Hardy said it without fail every time he left, but today, it was as if a house had fallen on me.

Riley, you're in charge.

I was in charge, not that I'd been doing a great job of it so far. I watched these people come and go every day and sat behind my desk, feeling helpless, wishing there was something more I could do. And here I was, with the perfect opportunity right in front of me. I was so focused on myself that I almost missed it completely.

The pennies!

At the end of the year, I would donate my savings to the American Cancer Society. I might not be able to be a scientist and find a cure, or be a nurse and ease suffering, but I could at least direct my small resources to someone who could. I felt more excited about this than any of my other previous ideas.

"Riley, what are you smiling about? Are you looking up porn on the Internet again?" Sarah said, trying to keep a stern mask on her face.

I didn't say anything but merely grinned wider. She cocked her head quizzically, raising an eyebrow.

"What is going on with you? If I didn't know you better, I'd say you were in love."

I laughed at that. "Nothing could be further from the truth," I said slyly.

"You are! Is it that new guy in the lab?"

I stayed silent, still grinning like an idiot.

"Well, if you're not in love, then you have a secret. And no one keeps a secret in this office for long. Good luck."

She wandered back into a room with a chart, and I was left with only my happy thoughts. I took the seven pennies from my pocket and stacked them neatly in front of my computer, where I could see them.

I stood in the sweltering sun, wondering if it was hot enough in the dirt to melt my flimsy yellow flip-flops. Sweat beaded around my hairline, and a drop suddenly ran down the side of my face to my chin. Another quickly followed, this time ending up in my eye and burning like acid. I eyed the syrupy remains that had once been a lime Slurpee, now reduced by the heat to a sticky green puddle. I considered guzzling it anyway but changed my mind abruptly when I discovered the unlucky wasp floating in it. Drowning in a Slurpee on the hottest day of the year wasn't such a bad way to go . . . for a wasp.

I turned my attention back to my grandfather, who was digging a hole. His face was a mottled purple-red, and I worried that he might drop over suddenly in this oppressive oven. My grandfather had problems with his heart. I knew this because he had a scar on his chest—a long pink scar that he showed me once from one of his heart surgeries. I traced it with my little finger and asked him if it hurt; he assured me that it was all better now.

"Maybe we should go in and take a break for a while," I said timidly.

He didn't speak, just grunted what I assumed was a no.

"We can come back out later, when it's a little cooler. Or I can come back another day."

"Aren't you excited?" he asked, stopping to lean on the shovel.

"Of course I'm excited, but not if it makes you sick. Whatever it is, it's probably been there a long time. And it will still be there when the sun goes down, or even tomorrow."

He smiled a patient smile. "That's all the more reason to be in a hurry. Whatever is down there has been waiting in the dark, wanting to come up to see the world. I'm not sure how long it's been there, but it doesn't want to wait another day." He lifted the shovel, ready to drive it back into the ground, but I reached over and put my hand on his shoulder.

"At least let me dig for a while."

He passed me the shovel and sat down on the plastic deck chair he dragged into the dirt driveway when we started.

"Does Grandma know about the hole in the driveway?" I asked, struggling for breath as the sun bore down directly on top of me.

He waved his hand, brushing it off as unimportant. "We'll have our treasure, and she'll have her driveway back before you know it."

I counted to eight in my head while wrestling with the unyielding dirt. I will be eight tomorrow, I thought. As much as I wanted to be helpful, I really wasn't getting anywhere with the digging. I was much more useful in sifting through the dirt clods, checking for anything that might be lurking.

"Maybe we missed it," I said, trying not to sound as frustrated as I felt. The temperature did nothing to bring out my better side, and I kicked a clump of dirt petulantly.

Grandpa picked up the metal detector, bringing it to the hole. He made some minor adjustments before lowering it over the broken ground. The high-pitched whining was unmistakable as it hovered like an alien ship, inspecting the territory and announcing in a strange language that there were indeed signs of life.

"There's definitely something there. I can't understand why we haven't found it yet." He mopped the sweat from his face with an old rag he had tucked into the waistband of his pants, sighing loudly. "Well, back to work."

I didn't remember ever thinking of him as old until that moment. There was more of his life behind him than there was ahead, and the thought frightened me a little. But as quickly as I glimpsed his age, it passed. The years receded and he was the same old Grandpa he always was, humming to himself as he dug an unsightly pit in his own driveway.

I hoped that Grandma would stay busy with whatever was occupying her in the house, at least until we managed to retrieve the riches and fill in the hole. I felt quite lucky to be a partner in this quest and took my role very seriously, sifting carefully through the pile of dirt that was accumulating.

"Wait a minute—do you see something shiny, or is it just my eyes playing tricks in this heat?" Grandpa asked, stooping forward to peer into the hole. I thrust my hands into the earth in the vicinity of a small glint I could barely see. Crumbling through the mass, I was left with a thin copper coin. My mouth formed a round O, and I couldn't seem to close it. This was more magical than I could imagine. The strange coin was about the size of a penny, but it was unlike any penny I'd ever seen.

"What is it?" I finally managed to spit out.

Grandpa took it from my hand, turning it over and squinting at both sides. "Well, I'll be," he said, shaking his head. He used his sweat rag to polish the coin, looking quite pleased.

"What? What is it?" I said impatiently, wondering why old people had to be so slow sometimes.

"It's an Indian Head penny—1903, it looks like. Even older than me," he chuckled.

I couldn't believe it. Things like this just didn't happen, except maybe in books. I felt the acute disappointment that comes with witnessing someone else's good luck, but at least I got to be there for the big discovery.

"Well, I think that this penny should be yours, since you found it."

"I didn't find it, not really. And you did most of the digging anyway," I said, looking at the ground.

"No, I insist. We'll drill a hole in the top so you can wear it on a chain around your neck."

I nodded, picturing myself showing it to all my friends at school. He dropped it into my waiting palm.

"Happy birthday, Riley."

chapter 4

If the reason for climbing Mt. Everest is that it's hard to do, why does everyone go up the easy side?

—George Carlin

W hen I got home from work on Valentine's Day, I was all ready to settle in for the evening. I had a tradition on Valentine's Day, a holiday that was right up there with New Year's Eve as far as I was concerned. As soon as I got home, I changed into comfortable pajamas and my favorite ratty old slippers. I started the festivities with way too much chicken lo mein from my favorite Chinese restaurant, which I chased down with a pint of Chunky Monkey while watching *Somewhere in Time*. Depending on how depressed I was already, sometimes I would stop the movie before Richard got sucked back into his own era, so they could have a happy ending. But I was determined to finish the whole movie this year. I guess it sort of has a happy ending anyway, because they're together . . . except they're both dead.

I was just getting the movie started when the phone rang. I hurried to swallow my mouthful of lo mein before picking it up.

"Hello?"

"Hi, is this Riley?"

"Yes?"

"This is James—Lauren's friend," he said, a hint of a Southern accent in his voice.

I really wasn't prepared for this tonight. I mean, that's a little presumptuous to assume that I'd be sitting home on Valentine's Day. I've really got to get caller ID.

"Hi, how are you?"

"I'm fine, thank you. I've been meaning to call before now, but I've been really busy."

"Yeah, Lauren said you were running a marathon. How was that?"

"I finished, which was really all I wanted. I didn't think I was going to win or anything."

"I always wanted to run a marathon just so I could say I did it, but I have . . . bad knees," I finished lamely. *Nice, Riley—what are you, seventy-five?*

"No kidding. Well, what are you doing Saturday night?"

"Um, I think I'm free."

"I thought maybe we could go shooting."

I laughed maniacally at this suggestion. At least he has a sense of humor.

Only he wasn't laughing.

"Shooting?" I managed to squeak out, my voice deciding to jump an octave.

"Sure. Have you ever been?"

I am almost a vegetarian. I eat a little chicken and some turkey, but that's as far out as I get. No cow. No pig. No fish. And the idea of killing something makes me want to run and hide. I suddenly pictured James's house, with stuffed deer heads and other scary taxidermy-type items peppering the walls. Can you imagine if you were a taxidermist? I'd be afraid that those poor animals would come alive in the middle of the night, looking for payback.

"Riley? Are you there?"

"Sorry, I guess I zoned out for a minute there. I've never been shooting. What do you shoot exactly, because I'm not sure I could kill anything."

He laughed. "How about a target? Or would that be too sad?"

I've always loved FBI shows—the *X-Files* is my favorite. I had a sudden vision of pulling my Sig Sauer from its holster, looking as dangerous as Scully. Maybe I'd be really good at shooting. Then again, maybe it would be like bowling. Would I get involuntary manslaughter for accidentally shooting James, or would I get murder one?

"Well, I guess I could shoot a poor, defenseless target if I had to."

"Great. I'll see you Saturday at 7:00, okay?"

"Looking forward to it," I said sweetly.

It's a good thing I'd be learning how to use a gun, because I wanted to *kill* Lauren. I went back to the couch and my lo mein, which was cold, and started the movie.

. . . .

Besides the whole James debacle, the night was going as well as could be expected. I was almost to the part in the movie where I usually stop it—Christopher Reeve pulls the penny out of his pocket and realizes he's starting to disappear—when suddenly, someone's car alarm started going off in the parking lot. Between the screeching alarm outside and Jane Seymour screaming, "Richard, Richard, RICHARD!" over and over, I was a little freaked out. I looked at my watch—11:36. I pushed pause on the remote and wandered over to the window. I peeked through the blinds.

In the parking lot below, I saw a guy sprint to his car, carrying a beautiful bouquet of roses. It was hard to tell, but it looked like he was fumbling to find the right key. He finally managed to disable the alarm and leaned against his car to catch his breath. Just when I was about to go back to the movie, he swung around, wielding the bouquet like a weapon, and began savagely attacking his car with it. He kept at it until there was nothing left but red petals on the ground. Then he wandered off into the dark. I didn't know whether to laugh or call the police. Finally—someone who was having a worse Valentine's Day than I was.

I turned off the TV and made sure the door was locked. Maybe I would finish the movie next year. I slid under the covers and switched off the lamp by my bed. As I drifted off to sleep, I wondered what one might wear to go shooting. Kevlar?

. . . .

"Shooting? He's taking you *shooting?* As in, with a gun?" Sarah asked in disbelief.

"As much as I'd like to believe there's another kind of shooting, I'm fairly certain a gun is involved."

"Is he crazy? You don't take your blind date shooting . . . unless you're a serial killer."

"Trust me, I've considered the possibility," I said dryly.

"So you're just going to let this total stranger drive you up into the mountains somewhere with a couple of guns?" she demanded.

I was alarmed. "I assumed we were going to a shooting range with other people around, but he didn't really say." I paused, considering this new, disturbing possibility. "I'll have my cell phone with me—it will be fine," I said, hoping I sounded calmer than I felt.

"Well, at least call me when you get home. So I know you're safe."

"It might be really late."

"I don't care. I can't sleep if I'm picturing you running for your life in the woods."

"Thanks. I feel so much better. Actually, it could be worse. You should have seen this psycho in my parking lot last night." I told Sarah and Kate, who just walked in, about the mystery flower-killer, and we laughed until there were tears running down our faces.

. . . .

I talked to my mom at lunch. She called to tell me that Mitch lost both his front teeth yesterday. She only found one under his pillow though, so she asked him the next morning how much money the Tooth Fairy left him. He told her a dollar, and she said that didn't seem like enough for two teeth. He explained that he only left one, and when she asked him why, he said that one dollar was plenty for now and he was saving the other tooth for when he really needed the money.

When there was a pause in the conversation, she said, "I've been wondering, Riley—what did you end up choosing as your resolution?"

I suddenly felt shy, and my face turned red. "I decided to save all my pennies, and at the end of the year I was going to buy something fun."

"That's a really good idea. How are you doing?"

"I don't have enough for a new BMW yet, but it's coming along."

"See—I knew you could do it."

"Well, I've decided not to buy something. I'm going to donate the pennies to cancer research instead."

"Riley, that's a wonderful idea," she beamed.

"I feel good about it, Mom, like I'm actually doing something important. Thanks for forcing me to be good," I said jokingly.

"Honey, I just made sure you got started. It's your good idea. I would never have come up with something like that. I'm sure you have to get back to work. Call me and let me know how your date goes, okay?"

I told her I had a blind date, but I figured it was wiser to leave out the whole shooting part until afterward. No use in worrying her unnecessarily.

"I will. Love you, Mom."

"Love you too, Riley."

. . . .

6:47. I put my lipstick on with a shaky hand and wondered again why I hadn't just called to cancel. I tried to call Lauren a couple of times earlier to see how much she really knew about this guy, but she was conveniently unavailable. She was famous for losing her cell phone, leaving it somewhere odd until the battery went dead. One time it took her a week to find it.

I heard a knock on the door and hurried to open it. I took a deep breath, stifling the impulse to answer it with a frying pan poised behind my back. I opened the door tentatively to reveal a tall, good-looking guy with a killer (though I hoped not literally) smile.

"You must be Riley," he drawled.

"I hope so," I said, smiling. The accent was actually kind of cute, but now I had something else to worry about. I have this fear of subconsciously picking up the accent of anyone I'm talking to. It's not the strangest phobia I have. When I was a little girl, I used to be afraid that when the hymn was over at church, I would lose control of the volume of my voice and just keep singing. You laugh, but if you'd ever heard me sing, you'd understand the panic.

"I hope you're not too disappointed, but the shooting range is already closed."

The stress, which was simmering all day just below the surface, melted out of my pores, creating an invisible pool on the floor in front of me.

"Oh, darn," I said, grabbing my purse on the way out the door.

Maybe there is hope for you yet, James.

"So I thought we'd go line dancing instead."

Maybe not.

. . . .

We had a nice dinner at a Mexican restaurant across from a club with a giant banner strung across its pillars, announcing that there was COUNTRY LINE DANCING TONIGHT!!! James seemed to be an okay guy. He came here from Tennessee on a football scholarship and liked it so much he decided to stay. He liked sports (no big surprise there), he loved his dog, Snoots, and he missed his family. He also had soulful brown eyes, showcased by the longest eyelashes I'd ever seen on a man. I wondered if the guys on his team had teased him about it.

After dinner we headed to the club, the tacos and the excess stomach acid combining to burn a crater in my stomach. I put my best foot forward (no pun intended), but it must have been obvious to James that line dancing wasn't my thing. He was really sweet and patient though, trying to teach me the one thing you either have or you don't—rhythm.

When a slow song started, I panicked. His arms snaked around my waist, and I awkwardly put mine somewhere in the vicinity of his shoulders. I was holding myself so stiffly it must have been like dancing with a mannequin. I leaned in a little toward him, fearing everyone might think we were brother and sister if we didn't stand a little closer. He leaned in a little as well, and for a moment I was afraid he was going to kiss me. But he bypassed my mouth and went straight to my ear.

"You know, you'd be having a lot more fun if you'd just relax a little," he whispered.

Before I knew what I was saying, I blurted out, "I know—I have control issues."

He laughed a little at that, and I tried unsuccessfully to will my muscles to loosen up before I caused any serious damage. The song ended, and I was surprised to see that it was the last song of the evening. James dropped me off and we shared a quick awkward hug and the compulsory, "This was fun—we should do it again sometime."

I made the promised call to Sarah, telling her that everything was okay, since we decided to leave the guns at home. After that, I was still too wired to go to bed right away. So I sat on the couch and flipped through the TV channels. I saw that commercial for Paxil at least three times. You know—the drug that's supposed to make you less frightened about mingling in social situations. I'm guessing it probably wasn't a coincidence.

I was starting to get a little drowsy when my cell phone rang, startling me awake.

"Are you home from your date? I didn't want to call you too early," Lauren said excitedly.

"Yes, I'm back, no thanks to you. Where were you earlier when I needed you?"

"I couldn't find my phone. Somehow it got wedged under the seat of my car. Was something wrong?"

"Well, when your blind date wants to take you shooting, you

like to check with the person who set you up. It would have been comforting to know that he didn't have an extensive criminal record before we went out."

Lauren absolutely howled with laughter. "That's so funny. Now that you mention it, I think he's taken other girls shooting before. I'd forgotten all about that," she said, her voice strangely reminiscent.

"I'm glad you're enjoying this. If you think it's so amusing, maybe you should go out with him."

"Even though it's legal to marry a distant cousin, I don't think he's the guy for me."

"I can't believe it. You're actually related?"

"Somewhere down the line. James explained it to me once, but I couldn't follow the trail. Some of the names he mentioned were people I didn't even know."

"Speaking of the guy for you, how was traffic school last night?"

She paused, and I could tell she was replaying the evening in her head. "There's something about him. He's really different than anyone I've ever met."

"Different good or different bad?"

She giggled. "He's so serious. There were about fifteen other people in the class, but I swear he kept staring at me, and then he'd catch himself. He'd get this stern, determined look, and then he would focus his attention on somebody else. It was almost like he was punishing himself for ogling me!"

"This is so exciting!"

"Why is that exciting?"

"Because he likes you, and you like him! He's obviously just very shy. Don't you see—this could be it; he could be *the one!*" I squealed. "And you would have the perfect story to tell about how you met!"

"Well, unless I suddenly embarked on a new life of crime, I think that the chances of us meeting again are between slim and none."

"But you said . . . "

"It was a harmless flirtation, and I probably imagined the whole thing. My imagination does tend to get a little carried away. Remember the time I was convinced that random UPS guy in the elevator was my soul mate?"

I snorted.

"It will come to nothing," Lauren said firmly.

"We'll see," I said, yawning widely. "I'd better get to bed."

"By the way, you never said how you liked shooting. I hope you weren't a better shot than James—the quickest way to alienate a man is to outdo him at something. He only took you so that he could show off, you know."

"We didn't go. He took me line dancing instead."

"It just gets better and better, doesn't it? It's like he had a list of things that would annoy you . . ."

" . . . or a good informant."

"Good night, Riley."

"Night, Lauren."

chapter 5

All of us are born with a set of instinctive fears—of falling, of the dark, of lobsters, of falling on lobsters in the dark.

—Dave Barry

Ten days into March, I had barely passed the 400 mark. Before I started saving the pennies, it seemed that there were pennies everywhere I looked. Whenever I stuck my hand into my purse, hunting for change, I pulled up handfuls. But now that I was actually counting them, there weren't nearly as many as I thought. I was a little discouraged at my slow progress, and I almost regretted telling my mother about my big plan. At this rate, my contribution would be small indeed. It was embarrassing now, thinking about how excited I was about really making a difference. Still, I'm doing what I can, and that's better than nothing, even if it is small.

I hadn't heard from James since our date, which wasn't a huge shock. He was very sweet, but we just weren't a great fit.

"Don't worry about it. There's always another guy. Just look around you—they're everywhere!" Lauren said, in what I am sure was meant to be an encouraging tone. It was Saturday and we were eating giant chocolate chip cookies at the mall, taking a break from a hard day of shopping.

"I've noticed. They do seem to be everywhere, all calmly going about their business and paying absolutely no attention to me," I said glumly, licking a spot of melted chocolate from one finger.

"I've heard that the surest way to meet someone is to make a decision not to. Being happy with your current situation and trying to maintain the status quo, it's only natural that life would throw a wrench into your plans by putting Mr. Right smack into the middle of your path."

"Maybe that's why you met Stewart—because you weren't looking for him."

"I'm not sure Stewart qualifies as Mr. Right."

"Oh, wait a minute—I remember now. You were looking for something when you met Stewart, but it wasn't Mr. Right—it was your cell phone!"

"Oh, very funny." She took a long sip of her diet soda. "Guess what? I got pulled over again."

"You little speed demon! I wasn't serious when I suggested that you should drive like a maniac so you might have a chance to see him again."

"I've been a model driver since the last . . . incident, thank you."

"Seriously Lauren, if you keep getting tickets at this rate, I'll be spending my Saturdays visiting you in prison!"

"I didn't get a ticket!" she exploded.

"Well?"

Her porcelain complexion went from cream to bright red in seconds.

"Stewart tracked you down, didn't he?" I said triumphantly.

"He wanted my phone number so he could call and ask me out." By now, she was blushing furiously.

"Why didn't he just look it up at work? I'm sure they have access to things like that."

"He said he didn't feel right about using it to call me without my permission."

"Wow. Either he actually has a conscience, or he knows just what to say to make girls think he's innocent and sweet."

"He seems so sincere. I think he might be the real thing."

"When are you going out?"

"Friday night."

"This is definitely promising. I think we should have another cookie to celebrate."

. . . .

I took a walk around the hospital grounds at lunch on Monday. It was one of those late winter days that is March masquerading as May. The sun comes out suddenly, so warm that you almost remember what spring was like. As I strolled outside, enjoying the blue sky and the unseasonably warm sunshine, I watched a girl about my age coming back to work from lunch on her motorcycle. She clutched a bag from McDonald's in one hand, her green scrubs peeking out from underneath her leather jacket. She leaned in close to the motorcycle, as if it were an extension of herself. I found myself in complete admiration and awe of her . . . coolness.

Judging from the looks that she was getting from the male population returning to work, I wasn't the only one. Maybe I needed a new image. However, imagining actually riding a motorcycle made me break out in a cold sweat, besides the fact that I was fairly certain I wasn't equipped with the level of cool necessary to pull it off. How was it possible that we were both wearing scrubs, yet she was still much cooler than me? Maybe it was the jacket.

I headed back into the office, taking one last look over my shoulder at the beautiful day I was leaving behind. When I got inside, Stacey was sitting in a chair, reading a magazine in between patients. She was always showing up to work with different colored hair, and today it was blonde with red and brown highlights.

We hardly ever work together, but I get along with Stacey really well. I think it's because we both have the same warped sense of humor. In fact, I think her ability to laugh at herself is one of the things that make her such a good nurse. Most days, she has an unbelievably funny story to tell. When I first met her, I would have sworn she was making them up. But I guess odd things just seem to happen to her—that's something else we have in common. Today was the first time I'd worked with her since my blind date with James, and she got a big kick out of his choice of activity. Of course, she couldn't resist sharing a bizarre tale of her own.

"Oh, I can top that. I actually went out with a guy one time who took me back to his place to see his bug collection: rows and rows of boxes with glass lids, full of dead bugs with pins sticking out of them. I've never been so creeped out in my life," she said, giving a little shudder.

"Stacey, do you think I'm cool enough to ride a motorcycle to work?" I blurted.

She choked on the chocolate milk she was drinking until I thought she might need the Heimlich. "You'd probably hyperventilate just strapping on the helmet. What made you come up with that?" she asked, interrupted by another bout of coughing.

"I don't know. I saw this girl coming back to work from lunch on her motorcycle, and everyone was staring at her. I guess I was jealous."

"Well, I don't think I'd run right out and buy one if I were you—it's not really your thing."

I scowled at her. "What about . . . horseback riding?"

"Didn't you tell me once that you were terrified of horses? Something about biting?"

"Look at their teeth! You can't tell me something with teeth like that might not suddenly turn on you," I said defensively.

"Yeah, hardly a day goes by that I don't hear about someone in the ER needing stitches due to a savage horse bite. How about . . . water skiing?"

"I get seasick on boats, and my balance is terrible. And then you fall, and you get water up your nose, and it burns."

"Skiing?"

"Same as waterskiing, only with broken bones instead."

"Rock climbing?"

"I don't like heights."

"Bungee jumping?"

"I'm not even going to dignify that with an answer."

"Skydiving? Bull riding? Big game hunting?" she teased.

"What do you think?" I said disgustedly.

She closed the magazine and leaned forward, her eyes sparkling with amusement. "Well, that clinches it. I'm afraid I'm going to have to diagnose you as being terminally uncool."

"I'm afraid of everything, aren't I?" I said, experiencing a huge revelation.

"Well, I didn't want to be the one to say it . . . "

"No wonder I'm not married, or even in a relationship. I'm probably subconsciously afraid of that too!" I said, the panic rising in my voice.

"Oh, come on Riley, I was joking. I'm sure you're not afraid of everything."

"I am! I'm terminally uncool!" I wailed.

"You are not. There are plenty of things you're cool enough for."

"Name one."

She hesitated, trying to come up with something good.

"Roller skating?" she said finally.

"That's it? Roller skating?" I didn't bother to tell her that I was a terrible roller skater—more like a roller faller. I usually spend more time sprawled on the ground than actually skating. By the time I'm done, I'm so gouged up that I'm an excellent candidate for skin grafts. "This is pathetic—I can't believe I've never realized this before."

"Riley, everyone has things they're afraid of," Stacey said helpfully.

"Yeah, *things*. Not everything."

"I'll bet you're not afraid of puppies," she said confidently.

I paused. "How big is this hypothetical puppy?"

Stacey sighed, and Sarah appeared in the doorway.

"Stacey, I need you to pick something up at the pharmacy for me, if you're not busy."

"Nope, just helping Riley come to terms with her inner demons. You'll be okay here by yourself, right?"

I made a show of looking around me. "I don't think there are any rogue bands of wild puppies around, so I should be just fine."

When Stacey returned, she set a huge scoop of cherry chocolate chip down on the counter by my arm.

"What's that for?"

"Well, I felt bad about teasing you, and I knew that ice cream was the best way to apologize."

"It isn't butter pecan, but I guess it will have to do," I sniffed.

"Riley?" she said between mouthfuls, looking thoughtfully at my latest stack of pennies.

"Yes?"

"Is there a reason behind this coin-stacking habit you've developed, or has your obsessive-compulsive nature finally taken over?"

"I guess a little of both. It started out as a way of getting around New Year's resolutions and sort of blossomed from there."

I told her about my current plans for the coins. I didn't intend to tell anyone at work, and I was afraid it sounded a little cheesy and lame as I heard myself saying the words. She considered my revelation silently for a minute, licking the ice cream from her plastic spoon. From one of the back rooms, an alarm beeped from one of the patient's medication pumps, indicating that some attention was needed. She threw away her Styrofoam cup, stopping in the doorway.

"I don't know quite how to tell you this, but I'm afraid that may be cool. Congratulations."

I grinned at her as she went off to investigate the malfunctioning pump.

. . . .

When I came into work the next morning, the first thing I noticed was a large piggy bank made of clear glass, its belly already looking comfortably full of pennies. There were several nurses sitting in their chairs, sneaking glances at me and trying not to smile.

"Does anyone know anything about this?"

I got nothing in response except a bunch of guilty looks.

"Stacey sort of told us about your . . . project," Sarah said finally. "We thought maybe we could help. Ice cream is ninety-six cents, you know."

I was confused. "What does ice cream have to do with it?"

"Change from a dollar for ice cream is four pennies. I'm always looking for a good excuse to eat ice cream."

Everyone nodded. "It's tough to do your part for charity, but we'll do our best," Kate chimed in.

I shook my head, laughing. "That settles it, then—we've gotta start eating more ice cream. You guys are great."

I sat down at my computer, looking at the happy glass pig, then at the nurses bustling around the office. I thought about how lucky I was to have friends like these. March was turning out to be a pretty good month for pennies.

chapter 6

One kind word can warm three winter months.

—Japanese proverb

I rolled over in bed and squinted against the bright sunshine that zapped me in the face. It took a minute for my brain to register that it should either be dark outside, or it should be the weekend. Unfortunately, neither of these statements was true. This thought jolted me into complete awareness, and I grabbed the alarm clock to see the bad news I knew awaited me. 8:45. Since I was supposed to be at my desk around 8:30, it was a given that I was going to be very late.

I jumped out of bed, getting one leg tangled in the covers. I managed to right myself, but before I could celebrate, I tripped on my glass penny jar. As I was falling, everything seemed to happen in slow motion, and I chastised myself for leaving it by the bed last night when I was done counting. I finally hit the ground with a thud. My palms took the worst of the fall, and I noticed in dismay that one of them was bleeding. I felt around in the carpet until I found something sharp protruding—probably a carpet tack. I washed my hands with soapy water, slapped on a Band-aid, and scurried into my last pair of clean scrubs, making a mental note to do laundry.

Pulling my hair into a quick ponytail, I grabbed my tennis shoes and the giant coin jar and scrambled for the car. I intended to take the pennies to the bank at lunch and cash them in. The count last night was 1003, a number greatly boosted by donations from the nurses at work. I flipped on the radio when I started the car. The guys on the station I listen to were taking calls about the best April Fools' pranks.

That's right—it was April Fools' Day. How appropriate.

. . . .

By the time I got to work, it was 9:35, and there was absolutely nowhere to park. I circled the lot for fifteen minutes and finally found a really good space in the patient parking. I slid into it and snuck into the building, hoping the gray van wouldn't catch me.

At the hospital, there's this security guard who patrols the parking lot in his gray van, trying to catch employees poaching the patient parking. Two weeks after I started working there, he busted me. The look on his face was so serious, I was just waiting for him to pull out the cuffs and take me downtown for questioning. I considered pretending that I was deaf, but this guy didn't look like he'd find that very amusing. So now I just save myself the hassle and park at the back of the lot like a good girl. Except this morning. I didn't see him as I rushed through the door, but I knew he was out there somewhere, lurking. Like Captain Ahab, searching for his elusive whale.

When I got inside, I crawled into my seat, enduring the cracks from everyone about my lateness. I told them about my unfortunate morning.

"You should get a tetanus shot," Sarah said immediately.

"I don't need a tetanus shot," I argued.

"Really? When was the last time you had one?"

"I don't know. Kindergarten?"

She rolled her eyes at me. "Riley, you have to get a tetanus shot. Trust me."

"Oh, you nurses are all the same—looking for any excuse to stick a needle into someone. I'll be fine."

"With the luck you've had today?" she said incredulously. "You should *sprint* to the hospital pharmacy to pick it up. I'll call your doctor and have him fax over the order."

I still wasn't convinced.

"I'll even give it to you. You won't feel a thing," Kate assured me, patting me on the arm. Kate is great at giving shots. She gave me my flu shot last year, and it wasn't bad at all.

"All right, I'll get the shot if it makes you all happy. I have to take some pennies to the bank at lunch and I'll pick it up on my way back. Satisfied?"

She nodded her head, drawing up a syringe for some other unlucky soul.

. . . .

Despite the awful beginnings of the day, I was really excited by the time I went out to my car at lunch. My jar of pennies was stowed safely in the trunk where I hid it this morning. I don't know why I bothered—who'd want to steal a bunch of change? The sad thing was the pennies were probably worth slightly more than my car.

I drove to the bank, playing the radio loud and feeling downright cheerful. I popped the trunk, retrieving my treasure and carrying it proudly through the door. Luckily for me, it wasn't crowded. There was only one other person in front of me. I hummed to the tune playing in my head, lost in my thoughts.

"Excuse me?" I heard a rather impatient voice say. I looked up sheepishly to see another teller standing in the next window. "I can help you over here."

I strode up to the window, smiling brightly. "I'm sorry—I just got distracted, thinking about what a nice day it is. It seems like ages since we've seen the sun. Don't you love that; when you think you can't stand one more day of clouds and snow and gloom, and suddenly, the sun comes out?"

"Yesss," he said, drawing it out, like he thought I was the village idiot.

I took my first good look at this guy, struck by the impression that I had seen him somewhere before. I scrunched up my face, trying to piece it together in my mind.

"Have we met? You look so familiar."

"I don't believe I've had the pleasure. Maybe you've seen me at the bank," he said, forcing a patronizing smile, but his adorable dimples weren't fooling me. I could sense his irritation bubbling just below the surface.

"I don't think that's it. I swear I've seen you before, but I just can't place you. I don't usually come inside the bank, but I couldn't exactly fit this in the drive-thru container," I said, heaving the massive glass jar onto the counter in front of me.

"What . . . is this?"

"It's pennies," I said matter-of-factly, giving him a conspiratorial grin.

The bank teller, whose name tag said Paul, lifted one eyebrow, having the uncanny effect of making me feel like I was back in elementary school and I'd been caught with a novel wedged into my math book. He was a full head taller than I was, making him seem even more intimidating. He didn't say anything, just studied the jar from every angle, careful not to actually touch it. When he finally looked up again, you'd have thought I'd dropped a dirty diaper on the counter instead of a bunch of money.

"You *must* be joking," he said finally.

My hands started getting sweaty, but I tried to cover by flirting with him a little.

"Don't you guys have a big machine in here somewhere I could just pour these into? You know, where it sorts them really fast and spits out the bills?" I asked with an innocent look. It never hurts to play stupid and to flirt, but all it took was a look to know that he wasn't buying it.

Suddenly, his face split into a wide grin, the first sign of humanity I'd spied in him thus far. "Did Jack send you? He did, didn't he? This is an April Fools' joke! You almost had me. I don't know how you kept a straight face, hauling around that ridiculous container of pennies."

I was through humoring this good-looking but unpleasant man.

"I don't know any Jack, and this isn't a joke. I just want the cash for these 'ridiculous' pennies so I can get back to work," I said hotly.

"Well, this isn't the local grocery store. We don't accept loose coins. I'm sorry, but if you want to exchange your . . . pennies, you'll have to roll them in these first." He reached under the counter and pushed across a stack of paper coin rolls.

"Fine, I will! I mean, I'm just bogged down with free time. It should only take me, what, three days to roll them; maybe even less if I skip meals and give up sleep. Maybe I should just call in sick tomorrow."

I snatched the paper rolls off the counter, stuffing them into my bag and glaring at Paul the teller. I grabbed my coin jar and lugged it toward the door.

"I'll be back," I growled over my shoulder.

"Can't wait," he hurled back.

As I was almost to the door, I heard a little scuffle behind me.

"Just a minute, miss," he said suddenly.

"Yes?"

"Have a nice day," he said mockingly.

A strangled sound escaped from my throat, sort of a cross between a scream and a growl, and the teller next to Paul actually ducked. I felt guilty then—I didn't mean to scare him. I guess you really shouldn't make threatening sounds like that in a bank, but he's lucky that's all I did. It took every bit of self-control I had not to run back in and chuck the glass bank at him. I put the pennies back in the trunk and slammed it as hard as I dared. I spent the drive to work going back and forth between thinking about how good looking he was and wishing he would drown in a large vat of loose coins.

. . . .

I almost forgot to pick up the tetanus at the pharmacy on my way back, and I was still fuming when I walked into the office. I flopped into the chair next to Sarah, shoving the vial of serum across the counter.

"What happened to you?"

I massaged my temples with my fingers, trying to ward off the headache I felt brewing.

"Do you believe in reincarnation?" I said absently.

"What? Why?"

"Because I didn't before, but I just met someone I am positive will be spending his next life as a cockroach."

She snorted. "Who's your new friend?"

"Oscar the Grouch's less jolly cousin Paul just assisted me at the bank. Guess what's still in the back of my car?"

"Please don't say Paul."

I smiled. "No, it's not Paul—just a thousand pennies, give or take. Apparently, I have to take them home, and I'm not to come back until they are neatly counted into these handy paper rolls."

Sarah gave me a sympathetic look. "Well, on a happier note, are you ready for your shot?"

"What happened to Kate?" I asked nervously.

"Kate had to go home early, but she made me promise to take good care of you."

"I don't know about this," I said, rolling up my sleeve. It was at that inopportune moment that Celeste bustled through the door, carrying a stack of blankets and pillowcases. Celeste is one of our nurse's aides. She's very enthusiastic and sweet but not the sharpest knife in the drawer. She's going to nursing school, and lately she's been using us all as guinea pigs for various procedures. Last week, she got Kate to agree to let her try a blood draw. Kate's arm is still undergoing color changes—it's currently a nasty purple-green.

"Riley, what are you doing?" she asked eagerly.

"Sarah's going to give me a tetanus shot, aren't you, *Sarah?*"

"Yup, I'm just drawing it up now." She walked behind Celeste to get a syringe from the cupboard. Once she was behind Celeste, she began emphatically mouthing, "No! NO!"

"Oh, can I do it, Riley? Please?"

I hesitated a moment, but I knew there was no way out now. Everyone was going to have to take a turn being abused by Celeste, and if it wasn't this, it might be something worse.

"All right, all right," I said finally. "Just hurry and get it over with so I don't have to think about it. I'm not great with needles." I was glad that Stacey wasn't there to add one more item to the list of things Riley can't cope with.

"That's okay, I'm not great with needles either," Celeste said in a chirpy voice.

Sarah just stared at me, shaking her head as she handed Celeste the syringe.

"I really do appreciate this, Riley," she said, scrubbing my arm with alcohol. "I'll never be a good nurse if I don't get the chance to practice."

"But you have done this before, right?" I asked desperately.

"Sure—I gave this same shot to an orange yesterday."

. . . .

"Where did you get that wicked bruise?" Lauren asked.

I stuffed my clothes into the washing machine rather violently. "It's such a long story. Just one little part of the really rotten day I've had. I was duped into letting Celeste give me a tetanus shot. She didn't bother to tell me until afterward that I was the only thing she'd ever given an injection to that wasn't . . . fruit."

"So that's what got you out of sorts?"

"Why do you think I'm 'out of sorts'?" I asked, a little too harshly.

"Well, I'd say this washing machine was taking the brunt of the punishment, but you're definitely fixating on something else. Everyone has to start somewhere, you know," Lauren said, motioning to my arm.

"Oh, Celeste was just the icing on the cake," I grumbled.

"Who is it you wish you were pummeling, then?"

I groaned and jammed more clothes into the machine. "There was this guy at the bank today—Paul," I said, cramming the laundry in as tight as I could.

"I get the feeling we don't like Paul."

I could never stay angry for very long around Lauren. "Now

that is an understatement."

She separated her lights and darks into two machines, wait-ing for me to elaborate. The more I thought about it, the angrier I got all over again.

"And what did Paul do to land himself the place of Public Enemy Number One?" she prodded.

I started feeding quarters into the machine as I related my bank experience from earlier. Lauren's freckled face was furrowed with confusion by the time I finished.

"I don't get it. Are you mad because he wouldn't take your pennies, or because he didn't flirt back?"

"It had nothing to do with flirting!" I exploded. "He just didn't have to be such a jerk about the whole thing."

"But you did think he was sexy."

"He might have been cute, but he had the personality of a pitted olive. I couldn't care less whether he was interested or not." Since we were the only ones in the laundromat, we sat down cross-legged on a long table for folding clothes. We usually played UNO to kill time while we waited for the washer. I shuffled the deck and dealt. "Maybe we should just change the subject. How was your day?"

"Wonderful," Lauren said dreamily. I glared at her, as if she were saying it just to spite me. "Well, you asked." We played fast, the flurry of cards falling expertly from our hands into a pile.

"And how is Stewart—could he be the reason for your won-derful day?"

"He surprised me and showed up at work to take me to lunch . . . in uniform," she said, raising an eyebrow.

"What number date is this?"

"Number six," she said in a monumental tone.

"I bet all the girls made catty remarks about you after you left."

"Why would they do that?"

"Because you're so happy; it would only be natural for them to be jealous."

She hesitated with her card poised in mid-air, the game momentarily on hold. "You're not jealous, are you?"

"Of course I'm not jealous. You're my best friend, and I want you to be happy."

I really was only the tiniest bit jealous.

"UNO," she said, slapping down her second to last card.

I heard a strange sloshing sound behind me, and I whirled around to find my washing machine flooding soapy suds onto the floor.

"I tried to tell you that you were packing it too full," Lauren said, shrugging her shoulders and trying to stifle a giggle.

chapter 7

Some cause happiness wherever they go;
others whenever they go.

—Oscar Wilde

Over the past few days, I'd rolled a handful of pennies here and there when I had a minute, but I really wasn't getting anywhere. I decided that I would never finish if I didn't take some time to sit down and just do it. I sat on the rug in front of the television, flipping through the channels until I found an old Humphrey Bogart movie. Once I focused my attention on the coins, it really didn't take me that long. Not that I would ever tell Paul that.

Hmmm . . . Paul. I wondered if he was always such a crab. Maybe he was just having a bad day. Everyone has a bad day now and then. I watched as Humphrey Bogart swept Lauren Bacall off her feet. I wondered if he ever had a bad day.

When I was done, I leaned back against the couch and watched the rest of the movie, basking in the feeling of accomplishment that comes with completing a task that seemed insurmountable when you began. The current count on the pennies was 1,562—all were safely accounted for and rolled except the last twelve, and they went back into the glass bank.

As I pulled into the parking spot at the bank the next day, I realized that my heart was racing. I don't deal with confrontation very well—in fact, I'd go a mile to avoid a fight. Maybe I should just find a different bank.

My first impression was one of extreme relief, knowing I wouldn't have to face Pompous Paul again. But this was quickly followed by anger and indignation. I didn't do anything wrong; it's not like I started it. Why should I have to go through the whole impossible process of changing over my accounts to another bank? There was no way I was going to give him the satisfaction of knowing he'd run me off. I wasn't going to cower like a beaten dog. Riley Madsen was nobody's doormat!

I felt pretty good now. I was firing on all cylinders, ready to not only take anything he could dish out, but throw it right back at him. I grabbed the plastic bag full of penny rolls and lugged it into the bank lobby, prepared to do battle if necessary. I trudged up to the desk, looking around warily for Paul. Instead, I was greeted by a smiling girl whose tag said Kimberly.

"Can I help you?" she asked politely.

I lifted my bag of pennies onto the counter. "I just need to exchange these," I said, still glancing around and half expecting Paul to be lurking in the corner.

She pulled the bag over to her side of the counter. "You must have taken a lot of time and trouble to roll all these," she said sympathetically, sorting through the rolls.

"You have no idea."

She opened her drawer and took out a ten-dollar bill, a five-dollar bill, and two quarters. "Is there anything else I can do for you?"

"No, you've been very helpful, thank you." I tucked the money into my purse and headed for the door. On a whim, I turned around again. "Does Paul happen to be available?"

"He's not working today. Would you like me to give him a message for you?"

I smiled at her. I didn't imagine that she would be comfortable delivering the message I wanted to leave. "It's okay."

"Is he a friend of yours?" she inquired.

"Well, I've only met him once, but I feel I know him very well. He certainly made quite an impression on me."

She nodded her head. "Paul seems to have that effect on women."

I couldn't think of a response to that, so I just said good-bye and left. I got into my car, feeling oddly let down as I fastened my seat belt. I should have been elated that I managed to escape without having to justify my existence. But instead I felt deflated. I was all ready for a good fight. And what did that mean, anyway—"Paul seems to have that effect on women"? I mean, sure, he's handsome, but his manners could use some work.

My heart sank as realization washed over me. Kimberly must think I like him. She'll probably tell him a smitten girl with a bag of pennies showed up looking for him. On the other hand, maybe he'll be nice about it. You can't always trust your first impression of someone, right?

. . . .

After church on Sunday, I hopped in my car and drove home for Sunday dinner. I love Sunday dinner. There is nothing better than coming home to see your family, the air heavily scented with the smell of baking bread. This Sunday, my mother was cooking a turkey.

"What's the special occasion? Not that I'm complaining; I'll definitely be there," I said quickly.

"No reason—the turkey was on sale."

When I walked through the front door, I was met by an out-of-breath Mitch. He was still wearing his church clothes, only now his tie was around his head instead of his neck. He whooped and hollered, stopping briefly to tell me hello.

"Mitch, what are you doing?"

"I'm looking for Katie. Have you seen her?"

"I just walked through the door. How would I know where Katie is?" I said, trying not to stare blatantly at the couch, as I could see Katie hiding behind it.

"Well, if you see her, could you let me know?" he said seriously.

"Sure." I winked at Katie as I walked by nonchalantly. I arrived in the kitchen to find my mother and sisters hard at work.

Emily was washing lettuce for the salad, Olivia was opening a can of olives, and Charlotte was shaping the dough for rolls. My mother was stirring the gravy. I stepped up to a sink full of potatoes waiting to be peeled. I rolled up my sleeves and plunged into the potatoes and the conversation.

"How come Dad and Mitch and Katie don't have to help with dinner?" Charlotte complained.

"Katie's going to set the table, and Dad and Mitch get to do the dishes while we lay on the couch after dinner."

The idea that everyone had to take their turn at slave duty seemed to pacify Charlotte.

"So, Riley, Mom says you had a date the other night. How was it?" Emily asked breathlessly.

Emily is sixteen and at the age where romance is not only inevitable, but lovely. Olivia, who is fourteen, is close on Emily's heels. She has the same daft notions about love but without the opportunity to actually test them out. The fact that she isn't allowed to date yet is a bitter topic. As much as I try to convince her that she isn't missing anything, she refuses to believe me. And Charlotte is only ten, just entering the end of the "boys are icky" phase. As I told my blind date story, between the three of them, I had a rapt audience. At the end, Emily immediately said, "Are you going out again?"

"I don't think so. He hasn't called."

"That is just so tragic," Olivia said sadly.

I laughed. "My heart isn't exactly broken. He was a nice guy, but we just didn't fit," I explained. "I don't seem to be having much luck lately. You should have seen this guy at the bank the other day." I told them the Paul story, and at this point, any cooking had ceased completely. My sisters pulled stools from the bar, making a sort of semi-circle with me in the middle. They all laughed when I told the part about how I screamed and scared that poor teller. Even my mother, who tried to maintain a disapproving look, eventually relented, dissolving into giggles with the rest.

"So, he was really cute, huh?" Olivia said.

"Why does everyone keep saying that?"

"Well, I think he was really mean," Charlotte said. At ten, she worshipped me and would have agreed with anything I said.

"Thank you, Charlotte. Anyone else?"

"Maybe you could give it another shot," Emily said hopefully.

Mitch wandered into the kitchen, seeing us all standing around visiting.

"Aren't we ever gonna eat? I'm starving! Riley hasn't even finished peeling the potatoes yet," he wailed.

"You could always come in here and help her," my mother threw in.

"I don't wanna hang out with a bunch of girls. This house is full of women! I'll go see what Dad is doing." Out of the corner of his eye, Mitch spied Katie hiding under the kitchen table. "Ha!" he yelled, running toward her. She shrieked and scrambled down the back steps with Mitch hot on her trail, the door slamming behind them.

. . . .

"Well, girls, that was an excellent dinner," Dad stated, patting his belly.

It was an excellent dinner. When you live alone, you forget what it's like to sit down to a big homemade meal with other people. Most of my meals consist of something from the freezer section, various items in cans, or anything from the value menu at the drive-thru window. My stomach was unsure what to do with this quality or quantity of food, and I felt rather drowsy. Thinking about getting up and driving home was too much for me to contemplate yet, and I was happy just to sit and chat with my family.

It's funny how adults can sit around the table and talk for hours after a meal, but children get fidgety and anxious to be somewhere else. I could tell Mitch was reaching that point, pushing his leftovers around the plate. He took an extra roll and hollowed it out. He ate the soft middle, then filled the shell with some stray peas.

"We have something for you," he said mysteriously. He tried unsuccessfully to free the remaining peas that were lodged in his leftover mashed potatoes.

"Really?" I said, taking a sip of my water. "What could it be? A pony?"

He giggled and snorted at the same time. "No!"

"A . . . cactus? An . . . elephant? A . . . toaster?" Each thing on the list made him laugh harder.

"It's not any of those things. You'll see—we have a program."

I choked on my water, coughing and sputtering for a minute. I could tell that Mitch felt important, being privy to a secret I knew nothing about.

"A program?"

"Yeah, we want to help you." Charlotte elbowed Mitch, warning him that he couldn't elaborate any further without giving it away.

"Help me?" I had two strange realizations at the same time. First, I was repeating everything anyone said in an annoying, parrot-type manner. Second, I felt like I was on a TV show where the family and friends stage a surprise intervention for some poor, shell-shocked person. I wondered exactly what kind of help my family supposed I was in need of.

"Come on, everybody, you're scaring me a little."

My sisters and Mitch looked at each other, all of them scooting out of their chairs. They grabbed my arms and pulled me up, pushing me toward the couch and forcing me to sit. I found myself waiting for the words, "Riley, we all love you, but you have a serious problem . . ."

"Close your eyes," Olivia said excitedly.

I sat with my eyes closed until I felt something heavy being pushed onto the couch next to me.

"Okay, you can look now."

When I opened my eyes, I was surprised to see an old plastic ice cream bucket. I pried open the lid to discover hundreds of pennies. My siblings beamed, nearly bouncing with excitement.

"It's for your collection!" they said simultaneously. "We've been doing chores and saving them for weeks. Mom and Dad helped too."

This gesture was so wholly unexpected that I couldn't stop the tears that suddenly burned the corners of my eyes. I brushed them away quickly, holding out my arms for a group hug.

"You guys—this will help so much! Thank you." I pulled them all in around me, squeezing everybody tightly. I noticed that my mother was blinking away the tears as well, and my father was patting her on the back.

"All right, everybody, we're going to help someone else with their goal tonight too. Any guesses?" my mother asked.

Apparently the kids weren't in on this one—they all looked puzzled.

"Tonight for dessert, we will be serving . . . bubble gum ice cream!" Everyone looked at Mitch, who shouted, "All *right*! I've never had bubble gum ice cream before! I can cross it off my list!" He scampered off into the kitchen, no doubt eager to be first in line to try the exciting ice cream.

. . . .

When I got home, Lauren was sitting on my doorstep, clutching her pillow. Her eyes were red-rimmed and puffy.

"Lauren, what's the matter? Is everything okay?"

"Do you think I could stay here tonight?" she asked apologetically.

"Of course, but why? Did something happen?"

She tried to say something, but the words got caught in her throat. Tears started filling her eyes again, and she dabbed at them with a mangled tissue. With no other warning, she erupted into a squall of tears.

I took her arm and helped her to her feet. "Come inside and we'll talk about it."

I led Lauren to the couch, where I got her situated with a box of Kleenex. "Weren't you supposed to be on a date with Stewart tonight?" I asked encouragingly.

"Yes. Lucky number seven," she said between sobs.

"And?"

"It started out okay, but I should have known I was in trouble when Stewart was wearing a tie. He said he was taking me to the nicest restaurant in town."

"You went to Madeline's?" Suddenly, it all became clear to me. My eyes widened. "He didn't!"

"He did!" She reached into her coat pocket and retrieved a ring, depositing it into my palm with a shaking hand. It was a single solitaire diamond in a white gold setting, and it sparkled in my palm like fire. "It was nestled in the whipped cream on top of my raspberry trifle," she wailed.

"It's beautiful," I said quietly.

"It's insane!" she yelped. "What was he thinking?!"

"Well, obviously he was thinking that he loves you and wants to spend the rest of his life with you."

"Oh, how could he possibly know that? We've barely been going out two months now. I've had longer relationships with cheese."

"Now, be honest; weren't you even a little bit happy? You must have at least thought about it before."

"Sure, I've thought about marrying Stewart . . . eventually. I care about him a lot. But I wasn't expecting this now. Am I wrong to think this is too soon?"

"It is pretty quick," I admitted. "So, Stewart thinks enough of you to propose. The question is—how do you feel about him?"

"I don't know!" she exploded. "I haven't had enough time to figure it out yet. My head is spinning! I've waited for this day my whole life—why did it have to happen like this? I wanted to say yes because I was so excited, but I just couldn't. I told him I needed some time to think about it."

"There's nothing wrong with that." I turned the ring over in my hand before handing it back to Lauren. "It really is spectacular."

She sighed. "I know. I tried to give it back, but he said if I didn't want to marry him, he wouldn't have any use for it anyway, so I might as well keep it."

"That's so sweet."

"He seemed pretty disappointed. We hardly said two words to each other in the car. After he dropped me off, he kept calling my house. I think he was worried about me. I finally picked up the phone and talked to him long enough to let him know I was okay, but he wanted to plead his case, and I'm just not ready. I told him I'd give him a call after I had a chance to figure things out, and we said good night. I kind of thought he'd call back again."

"Didn't you just say you asked him not to keep calling you?"

"I know, but after we hung up, I felt so sad, like something was missing, you know?"

"Maybe that's your answer."

She shook her head. "No, the whole thing is crazy. I can't think about it anymore tonight. Is it really okay if I stay here?"

"I wouldn't let you go home, even if you wanted to. I think you're in need of some major cheering up, and I know the perfect thing. It just so happens that I have some chocolate chip cookie dough in the fridge—that always puts a smile on your face."

Lauren attempted a weak smile but only succeeded in looking like a heartbroken puppy.

"That was pathetic. You're going to have to do better than that." I handed her the remote. "You find us something to watch. I'm going to get the snacks."

We ended up having a slumber party on the floor in front of the TV, eating popcorn and cookie dough, flipping back and forth between an *Everybody Loves Raymond* marathon and the home shopping channel until we crashed. As I drifted into dreams, I thought back to the weight of Lauren's ring in my palm. I was only a little jealous.

chapter 8

I must warn you that when you finally have the pleasure
of saying the thing you mean to say at the moment you
mean to say it, remorse inevitably follows.

—Tom Hanks, *You've Got Mail*

With my family's generous contribution, it was nearly time to make another trip to the bank. I was starting to almost enjoy rolling the pennies. It was one of those great tasks that required very little active brainpower. It gave my mind a chance to wander off on its own, which was a nice change from work. I was amazed when I counted the pennies and discovered that the new grand total was 2,298.

I couldn't believe how many people wanted to help. Lab techs that came in to pick up our specimen started emptying their pennies into the office pig. There were people in various capacities in and out of the office all day—delivering the mail, bringing lunches from the cafeteria for the patients, and distributing the clean linens, and all of them seemed to have spare change that they willingly donated. Word spread, and sometimes the people dropping off the pennies didn't have any reason to come in, other than they wanted to be involved.

When I went to pick up the ice cream one day, the woman ringing me up added a large white Styrofoam cup full of pennies to my tray. I looked at it for a moment, not comprehending.

"You are the Riley that works in the Cancer Treatment Center, aren't you?"

"Yes," I said dumbly.

"The staff in the snack bar pooled these for your fund. I hope they help—it's a wonderful thing you're doing. My mother had breast cancer. She was too young when she died. I'd like to think that I helped to find a cure for someone else's mother," she said, her voice shaking.

I put my hand gingerly on her arm. She looked like she was going to cry. "Thank you so much." I didn't know what else to say, so I scurried out the door. I got to the end of the first hall before I had an idea. I turned around and went back to the snack bar. The woman was still at the register. She was wearing the most enormous pair of hoop earrings I'd ever seen. I glanced at the name on her badge.

"Paula? How'd you like to be my partner in crime?"

"What can I do?"

"Do you think you could find out who does the ice cream ordering?"

"That's easy—I order all the food for the snack bar," she said, puzzled as to where I was going with this strange question.

"Do you think you could talk to the supplier about donating enough ice cream for a one-day fund-raiser?"

"I guess it wouldn't hurt to ask. As long as the hospital agreed, we could put the proceeds from one day of ice cream sales toward your fund." I could hear the excitement building in her voice. "I'll call them as soon as I get a chance. I'm sure that when they hear it's for charity, they'll be happy to help."

"And we can make posters and put them up in the hospital, so everyone knows about it. At 100 pennies a head, we could make a fortune," I said, mentally trying to do the figures.

"Come in tomorrow and I'll let you know what I find out."

"If we could pull this off, it would be incredible!"

I went back to my desk and smiled at everyone who came through the door. I decided not to tell anyone in the office about the new plan until I found out whether Paula could sweet-talk the distributors. Everyone just assumed my good mood was because of the fudge ripple.

. . . .

I walked through the bank doors, full of peace and love for mankind in general. The sky was blue, the birds were singing, and people were basically good and kind. I carried my bag of pennies with a song in my heart; nothing was going to bring me down.

I saw Paul standing at the desk, and he actually smiled when he saw me. I forgot to breathe for a minute. He really was even cuter than I remembered. I walked straight up to him, putting my bag of penny rolls on the counter in front of him.

"Did it take you *that* long to roll those coins?" he asked, smirking.

"I've already been back since then. These are different pennies," I said, a bit huffily.

"Yes, I heard you came in looking for me," he said, ego just oozing from his voice.

"I wasn't looking for you. I was bringing back the pennies you wouldn't accept before."

"But you did ask for me. And you even remembered my name. I'm impressed."

"Bad impressions leave their mark, just like good ones do. I did remember your name, but not exactly fondly."

"Really? Would you be surprised if I told you I remembered your name as well?"

"What is it, then?"

"Riley," he said smoothly.

Actually, I was a little impressed. Even if he remembered me as Riley the Crazy Penny-Toting Girl, he still managed to come up with my name. I looked at the floor, trying to decide if I should wipe the slate and give him another chance—forgive and forget. My eyes landed squarely on the badge hanging innocently around my neck. I must have forgotten to take it off before I came in. RILEY, it said, in letters he couldn't possibly miss.

"You didn't remember my name. You read it off my badge," I said, frowning.

"Yes, but you still knew *my* name," he said, grinning cockily.

I felt the anger starting to bubble up all over again. Who did this guy think he was, flirting with me now? What made him think I would just melt and forget about everything that happened? When I didn't say anything, he must have taken that as a sign that I was caving.

"I think we may have gotten off on the wrong foot. Maybe we could start again," he said confidently, turning on the charm.

"You've really got some nerve. The last time I was in here, you treated me like something you found on the bottom of your shoe. And now you want to be my buddy? I don't think we have to be friends. Since I have all this change neatly sorted for you, you can exchange it for bills, and I'll be on my way."

His face fell and he looked away quickly, like he was trying to compose himself. He reached into the drawer and very precisely counted the money back to me with clenched teeth. By now, I was feeling incredibly guilty. Something inside me just couldn't make peace with him. Maybe it was because he was so certain that I would.

"Is there anything else I can do for you, Miss Madsen?" he asked icily, his eyes the coldest blue I'd ever seen.

"No, thank you," I stammered.

He busied himself with a stack of deposits, and although I knew I should apologize or at least say something, I didn't.

. . . .

Back at work, I slumped down in my seat, going over the schedule and seeing which patients had arrived for their appointments. Mr. Hardy was on the list, but I must have been at the bank when he arrived. I walked into the back rooms to say hello, but I didn't see him in his usual chair. I took my seat at the computer, sighing loudly.

"Mr. Hardy is really late—do you think he's still coming?" I asked, trying to keep the worry out of my voice.

"He didn't look great last week. Maybe he's been admitted to the hospital," Kate commented.

"Well, maybe he just forgot. He's forgotten before. Do you think I should call him to reschedule?"

"Yeah, why don't you call him and let him know he missed his appointment. Tell him we'll find him a spot if he wants to come tomorrow."

I dialed his number, which rang about ten times. I almost hung up. I didn't want the phone bothering him if he was sleeping. The answering machine picked up, but it wasn't his voice; just an automated message. After the beep, I said cheerfully, "Hello, Mr. Hardy. This is Riley at the treatment center. Just calling to let you know you need to reschedule, since you missed your appointment today. Give us a call and we'll get you in another time, okay? Have a good day."

As I hung up the phone, I felt a little uneasy. I looked up his name on the hospital computer system, but he hadn't been admitted. I clicked on my Internet browser, going right to the obituaries with a lump in my throat. But he wasn't there either, and I heaved a heavy sigh of relief.

"Did you get him?" Kate asked absently.

"No. Answering machine."

Her eyes went to my computer screen, waiting for me to say the words.

"He's not in there," I said, clicking it off abruptly. The superstitious voice in my head said I was jinxing him for even looking there.

Kate nodded, sifting through the mess on her desk. "I'm sure he just forgot."

But she wasn't sure. I could hear it in her voice. Kate had been working at the treatment center for eight years now, and I was afraid I was starting to pick up on things she intuitively sensed. The bell on the door rang, announcing that there were other people who needed my attention. I pushed the thoughts away, pasting a smile on my face for the patients on their way in.

. . . .

Walking to the car that night, I couldn't believe how wiped out I felt. Between the excitement over the ice cream idea, the confrontation with Paul, and worrying about Mr. Hardy, my emotions had been up and down all day. I was so glad it was Friday—tomorrow I was definitely sleeping in.

My cell phone rang, and I managed to dig it out of my bag before I missed the call. "Hello?"

"I don't know if you're ready for this," Lauren said.

"Try me."

"So, I talked to Stewart finally. I called him last night and told him I wanted to talk, so he came over."

"How did it go?"

"Pretty well. I told him that I like him a lot, but I'm just not positive yet that he's *the one*."

"And did he fully grasp the importance of the concept of *the one*?"

"I think he understood. He said that he realized it was kind of fast but that he'd waited as long as he could. Riley, he said he knew the first time he saw me—that's why he was so flustered. He said he was sure that night."

"I don't know if that's incredibly romantic or really strange."

"I feel exactly the same way! But he said he's willing to give me as much time as I need to make my decision."

"You know, I thought guys like that only existed in movies," I said wistfully.

"Wait, it gets better. I went to lunch with him today. He told me to meet him at this little Italian deli he likes near the police station. So we had sandwiches, and we're just chatting about mundane things when suddenly this ancient little Italian man comes out of the back room, playing the accordion. He comes to our table and serenades us, at which time Stewart proceeds to ask me to marry him . . . again."

I gasped. "What did you say?"

"I looked into his eyes, gave him my sweetest smile, and told him no. And do you know what he did? He just shrugged and said, 'You can't blame a guy for trying.' "

"Oh, Lauren, I really like Stewart. When do I get to meet him?"

"He was just asking the same thing about you. I told him we'd all get together for dinner one night soon. Listen, I have to go, but before I do, how was your day?"

I didn't want to bring her down by recounting my disappointing scene with Paul. Besides, I didn't want to sound bitter and jealous, so I took a deep breath and smiled. "Fine. Couldn't be better."

"Wonderful! I'll talk to you tomorrow and we'll fix a night for dinner, okay?"

"Sounds great," I said, wondering where I managed to summon the enthusiasm. It wasn't that I didn't want to meet Stewart; I just never imagined that Lauren would get serious with someone before I did.

I hung up and sunk into the car seat, taking off my badge and hanging it on the rearview mirror. It was only when I took a good look at it that I realized something; although RILEY was printed on it large as life, my last name was not.

"*Is there anything else I can do for you, Miss Madsen?*"

chapter 9

The great use of life is to spend it for something that will outlast it.

—William James

The skies were dark and cloudy when I drove to work on Monday. I love the rain, especially in the summer. It makes me want to curl up on the couch with hot chocolate and watch movies all day. I was afraid that it would start pouring before I got into the building and I would get soaked, but there were no drops yet when the door closed behind me.

When I walked into the office, there was no one around. I printed off the schedule for the next day and started pulling the charts. Between that and the phones, I was so preoccupied that it took me a minute to see the note by my computer. I picked it up and read it quickly, feeling puzzled.

> Riley, when you get in this morning, could you come up to my office for a minute? Thanks, Andrea.

I frowned. Andrea is my manager. I wondered if I did something wrong. It was about then that Stacey wandered in.

"Hey, I haven't seen you forever! How's it going?" she asked, picking up the phone and dialing a number.

"Okay. I'll be back in a minute. I'm just going to visit with Andrea."

"Ooh, called into the principal's office," she said teasingly.

"Do you know something I don't?"

"Well, I probably know lots of things you don't. But I don't think any of them pertain to this particular situation." I gave her a dirty look.

I felt a little nervous as I approached the door to Andrea's office, which was closed. Andrea was, as far as I could tell, a nice person and a good boss. But her time was mainly occupied with administrative stuff, and I hardly ever saw her. What could she possibly want to talk to me about?

I knocked tentatively on the door, hearing only a muffled response. I cracked the door open and peeked around the corner. She was sorting through some papers on her desk.

"Hello, Riley. Come in and sit down." She didn't look angry, so I took that as a good sign.

"I didn't see your note first thing, but here I am."

She smiled at me easily, resting her perfectly manicured hands on her desk. "How are you?"

"I'm just fine," I said edgily. I wasn't sure where all of this was going, but I was fairly certain she didn't get me in here to shoot the breeze.

"That's good. You've been here just over a year now, right?"

"Yes."

"Are you happy here?"

"Sure. I like the patients and the nurses—it's a good job."

"I just wanted you to know that I heard about what you're doing with the pennies, and I think it's wonderful. What a nice idea."

"Thank you. It's really snowballed from where it started. I'm afraid my original intentions weren't quite so selfless."

"Well, it really seems to be bringing everyone together, and I wanted to congratulate you." She paused for a moment, just looking at me. It was difficult for me not to squirm in my chair while she stared at me openly.

"I guess I'll get back to work, unless there's anything else . . ." I trailed off.

"There's just one more thing. One of the nurses brought this to me this morning." She pushed a newspaper clipping across her desk to me, and I sucked in a breath involuntarily as I read it. It was Wallace Hardy's obituary. Tears blurred my eyes, making it hard for me to read the words. Andrea pushed her box of tissue over to me as well, and her eyes looked sad.

"Sarah told me that you had become quite good friends with Mr. Hardy."

I nodded, not trusting myself to speak.

"The first patient who dies that you are close to is always the hardest. I didn't want you to find out in front of everyone else."

"Thank you," I managed to get out, hot tears streaming down my cheeks. I wiped them away with the back of my shaky hand, just wanting to be alone.

"It's good that you care so much, Riley. That's why we're here—to care for the patients. If we can help them to get better, that is the best possible outcome. But even if we can't, we can at least try to make this difficult part of their lives a little more bearable. To say that you have patients who are your friends is one way to know that you're doing your job the best you can."

I blew my nose and tried to smile at Andrea. I wanted her to know how much I appreciated her understanding.

"I thought maybe you might want to get out of here for a minute. Would you mind taking the office deposit to the bank for me?"

"Sure," I said numbly. I had taken the deposit to the bank once or twice before. I took the check from her hand and bolted for the door.

"Riley?"

I turned back, waiting for her to finish.

"It's never easy to lose a friend. But as time goes by, this will get easier for you—I promise."

I thanked her again and hurried out the door. Luckily, I didn't run into anyone on my way out. I probably looked like road kill. I ran down the steps and through the front doors into the parking lot. The rain was pouring now, but I didn't care. I just kept running until I got to my car, falling into the seat and resting my head on the steering wheel. I'm not sure why it hit me so hard. I guess I just assumed he would get better again.

I've always been this way about death. I could go to a total stranger's funeral and cry buckets. It's just easy for me to empathize with anyone's grief, and I tend to soak up any vibes of sadness that may be floating around, like a sponge. I remember a kitty I had when I was little—Oatmeal. She got hit by a car, and I thought the world was going to end.

And then there was my grandfather. When his last heart attack took him, I cried for days. I guess it comes down to the fact that I don't deal with change very well, and what is death if not the biggest change of all?

After cleaning myself up the best I could, I started the car and drove to the bank, pretty much on autopilot. The drive-thru line was massive. It would really be quicker to just go inside. It was only when I took the key out of the ignition that I realized I might run into Paul. I was in no condition to fight with him today, and I considered turning around and going back to work. But I did tell Andrea that I would take care of the deposit, so I decided to be brave and face him.

I took a look at myself in the rearview mirror. My hair was damp, and my eyes were red-rimmed and puffy. *Nothing like showing Paul what he's missing*, I thought, smiling in spite of myself.

I took one last look in the mirror before running into the bank, trying to avoid getting any wetter than I already was. There was only one person in front of me waiting, and I noticed with relief that there was one teller at the drive-thru and one at the desk, but neither was Paul. I thought back to when I left the message on Mr. Hardy's answering machine on Friday. Was he already gone then? The image of my voice, echoing through his dark, empty house was one of the saddest I could conjure.

The teller at the desk interrupted my sad reverie when he called out, "Paul, can you come out and help me for a minute?"

Paul stepped out from somewhere in the back, motioning to the man in front of me that it was his turn. I just stood there, praying that I would end up with the other teller instead. But Paul's customer was a very quick transaction, and before I knew it, I was taking those dreaded steps to his window.

"Hello, Riley," he said, not a trace of bitterness in his voice.

"Hi." I wished I were anywhere but there.

"No pennies today?" His voice was warm, not the sarcastic tone I was used to.

"Nope," I said, trying to smile. "Today is strictly work-related." I pushed the check and deposit slip to him, and his fingers brushed across mine briefly as he took it. He punched in something on the computer and handed me my printed receipt.

"Is anything wrong?" he asked softly. I was surprised to see the concern in his eyes. Like the icy exterior just melted away, revealing a person I'd never seen before. My next breath caught in my throat, and my heart pumped a little faster. My skin felt translucent, and I wondered if he could see right through me.

"Well, the short version is, I work in a hospital where they treat cancer patients. I found out this morning that one of my favorites didn't make it." I felt the tears brimming again and I cleared my throat, willing the tidal wave to subside.

"I'm so sorry. You must be a very good nurse."

"I'm not a nurse. I'm just a secretary."

"Well, you must be an even better secretary then, to care so much." His eyes were locked with mine, and it was out of my power to look away. I wasn't sure who this guy was, but I definitely liked him better than the old Paul. I knew there were other people in line waiting, and I finally had the good sense to break the connection.

"I'd better go—you have other customers," I said apologetically. "Thank you for listening." I took several steps toward the door before he said,

"Riley, wait. You forgot something."

I had the receipt and my car keys, so I didn't know what I might have forgotten.

He held up a red sucker. "These always cheer me up," he said with a lopsided smile.

I took it from his hand, feeling my insides melting.

. . . .

My eyes were still a little red when I got back to work, but the rain had stopped, and I felt a little better. I sat down in front of my computer and my email. There was one from Lauren telling me that we needed to go to dinner tonight because she had a surprise for me. She insisted that I meet her at Olive Garden at 7:00, no questions asked. I thought this all sounded very mysterious but replied back that I would be there.

Stacey appeared next to me, pulling up a chair to sit down.

"Are you okay?"

"I'm fine," I said, in a tone I hoped conveyed the fact that I really didn't want to talk about it. She wisely took the hint and didn't press the issue further, leaving me to my work.

While I was on the phone making an appointment for a patient, Kate answered one of the other lines.

"Riley, it's for you."

I switched over to the other line. "Hello?"

"Hello, Riley?"

"Yes?"

"This is Paula . . . from the snack bar?"

"Oh, hello! I'm sorry I haven't been over yet, but it's been one of those days."

"Don't worry about it. I just had some good news for you, and I was too excited to wait. Our supplier has agreed to donate as much ice cream as we can sell in one day, and the hospital has given the okay to have the fund-raiser. All you have to do is get in touch with human resources to set up a day!"

"Paula, you've worked miracles!" I wanted to get up and dance, but Kate was already looking at me strangely. "As soon as I find out the day, I'll let you know," I promised.

"Okay," she said, her voice full of excitement. We were like two girls planning a sleepover.

"Thanks again." I hung up the phone, noticing that all the nurses were hovering around as if they could sense that something was happening.

"What was all that about?" Kate asked.

I explained my idea about the ice cream fund-raiser to add pennies to the fund.

"Riley, that's brilliant! Everyone loves ice cream. You'll make a million pennies," Stacey beamed.

"Well, maybe not a million. But it certainly is stepping things up a notch, isn't it?"

"When's it going to be?"

"I'm not sure yet. I have to go to HR and get all the specifics ironed out."

"Get going, then," Sarah said, making a shooing motion with her hands. They all pushed me toward the door.

I walked across the hospital to HR, where a lady named Krista helped me. She decided that we should do the fund-raiser on August 17. The weather would be warm enough for ice cream, but it was still far enough out to get all the planning done. She gave me her card and told me to call her any time with questions or problems. Everything seemed to be falling into place.

. . . .

By the time I got to Olive Garden for dinner, I was absolutely starving. With all the drama of the day, I hadn't stopped to eat anything since breakfast. Lauren was already at a table, dipping breadsticks in Alfredo sauce.

"You have got to try this," she said, pushing the basket of bread toward me.

"It looks great, but honestly, at this point, even the tablecloth looks pretty good." I loaded up the warm breadstick with plenty of gooey Alfredo, closing my eyes as I bit down.

"Can you hear it?" Lauren whispered.

"Can I hear what?" I mumbled, my mouth full of delicious, cheesy bread.

"The angels singing," she said, looking around like she expected to see them circling over our heads.

"You're a goofball. But you weren't wrong about the bread-sticks."

I told her about Mr. Hardy and the good news about the fund-raiser. And I told her about the very odd encounter I had with Paul.

"Oh, Riley, he likes you! You're going to fall in love and get married and have twelve babies!" she cooed.

"Lauren, he doesn't like me. He was just being kind. I was surprised to discover he was actually human. I was starting to think that, under his clothes, he must have an on/off switch and a plug so he could recharge at night. In fact, after our last encounter, I was fairly certain that if we ever saw each other again, it would be too soon."

"Maybe you're an acquired taste, and it just took him a while to come around."

"I don't know whether that's flattering or insulting. Snails are an acquired taste."

"What about if I said you were one-of-a-kind?"

I smiled. "That's better. So, where is Stewart tonight?" I asked, retrieving a second breadstick from the basket.

"Working . . . and missing me. I was talking to him on my cell phone right before you got here."

"Any marriage proposals today?"

"Not yet, but it's early."

Halfway through the main course, Lauren sighed impatiently.

"What?"

"You haven't even asked about your surprise yet—that's not like you."

"I was so hungry, I completely forgot! What is it?"

She reached under the table, pulling out a large, beautifully wrapped box with a pink bow on top. Instead of trying to pick it up, she just scooted it toward me.

"What's this for?"

"You'll see."

I tore the paper off and ripped open the box underneath to find . . . another box. Lauren and I have been wrapping everything at least three times since we were twelve; it's sort of a tradition. By the time you get to the sixth or seventh box, it's hard to remember why we ever started it. I think it used to be funny.

People at the tables around us kept glancing over at the growing pile of boxes. The fifth box was a shoebox, and it was taped shut. I used my butter knife to saw through the tape, lifting the lid in expectation. The box was filled to the brim with pennies.

"Lauren, where did you get all of these?"

"I put a jar at the front desk at work, and people donated their change from lunch. Happy birthday!"

"What? What do you mean, 'Happy birthday'?" I said, puzzled.

Suddenly a group of waiters swarmed the table, setting down a round chocolate cake with one burning candle directly in front of me. My face turned a hundred shades of red as they all joined Lauren in belting out "Happy Birthday." When they finished, everyone clapped. I thanked them politely and blew out the candle. As they dispersed, Lauren busied herself dishing up the cake.

"Lauren?" I said sweetly.

"Yes?" She was careful to focus on the cake, avoiding my eyes.

"Did you tell them it was my birthday?"

"Yes." She licked the chocolate frosting from her fingers, still not meeting my gaze.

"Why?"

She looked at me finally, passing me a slice.

"I couldn't help myself. I really love this cake."

chapter 10

If you can't get rid of the skeleton in your closet, you'd best teach it to dance.

—George Bernard Shaw

The next few weeks were a blur, full of nothing but work and preparations for the fund-raiser. My mom planned a family night where we made posters to put up on the walls of the hospital. My sisters did the lettering, and Mitch spent hours cutting out circles of construction paper in every color you could imagine. He stacked them on top of each other until they were impossibly high, pasting them on paper cones to decorate the posters. He took his job very seriously. My family promised to stop by and get ice cream on the big day.

I managed to get the day off work so that I could help out at the ice cream table. We were going to set up in a little courtyard on the west end of the hospital, where the cafeteria sometimes hosted employee barbecues. The price for a scoop of ice cream was a hundred pennies, or a dollar, if that was all you had handy. The closer it got, the more nervous I was. What if it was a huge flop? What if there was a ton of donated ice cream left over? What if my office and family were the only ones who showed any interest? I knew that there was a buzz going around the hospital. Paula told me that several people asked her about it in the snack bar. But as far as actual numbers went, I really had no idea what to expect.

With Lauren's pennies and the latest batch from the office pig, the most recent total was 5,194. This was already more than I expected to have by the end of the year, and that was without any of the money we would make at the fund-raiser. I had more than enough pennies for another trip to the bank, but I had mixed feelings about seeing Paul again. I'm sure that he was just being nice, but part of me wanted to believe it was more than that. Despite our disastrous beginning, I started having these fantasies about us being an old married couple, telling our grandkids the story of how we met.

"Well, it wasn't exactly love at first sight . . . " Paul would say, patting my wrinkled hand lovingly.

I tried to tell myself not to get my hopes up, but every time I thought about him handing me that sucker, it was hard not to imagine that there might be something more.

So, I reasoned, I was just being friendly as I shaped the chocolate chip cookie dough into uniform balls, evenly spacing them on the cookie tray. Just because you make cookies for someone, it doesn't have to mean anything. It's just a polite gesture—like sending a thank you card.

. . . .

I smoothed my hair as I walked into the bank. Suddenly I felt self-conscious with a Ziploc bag of cookies in one hand and a bag of penny rolls in the other. *Maybe I should just peek around the corner first to see if he's here.*

I ducked behind the wall near the door, peering around it carefully. I could see Paul at the counter, smiling at the beautiful blonde girl he was assisting. She looked like she was one meal away from death. I wished that I wasn't wearing my baggy green scrubs. I probably looked like the Jolly Green Giant.

Something she said made him laugh out loud, his eyes twinkling as he threw his head back. She kept running her fingers through her silky hair, and he looked very much like he wanted to help her with it. I found myself getting more and more disgusted with him as I watched this pathetic display. Now she was laughing at something he said, and as she turned to go, she raised her hand in a little wave. He waved back, spotting me lurking around the corner. I panicked, quickly dropping the bag of cookies in the trash and sauntering up to the counter.

"Well, well, Miss Madsen . . . back again," he said, the tone of his voice indicating that he was highly amused. "You seem to be spending more and more time here. Tell me, do they pay you in pennies where you work?" His eyes glimmered like sapphires.

"I'm surprised you noticed me at all; you were so busy with your friend," I said smoothly.

"Yes, I saw you over there, spying around the corner. If I didn't know better, I'd say you were jealous."

"Right. Like I care who you flirt with. But I do have a question for you. Just out of curiosity, do they have to be blonde and brainless for you to show an interest?"

"Here we go—it always has to be a fight with you, doesn't it? What is your problem?"

"Problem? I don't have a problem."

"Well, you obviously think you're better than she is," he shot back.

"You know, after the last time I was in here, I thought we might at least be able to be civil with each other. But you've definitely got some issues. In fact, I'm going to suggest that they install an emergency Midol dispenser at the bank—'In case of severe mood swings, break glass,' " I snapped back. I slammed the bag down on the counter, and he grabbed it, a scowl on his face.

"I don't understand you," he said under his breath, counting the rolls of change.

"Obviously."

He shook his head, like I was some mental case he was humoring. I don't know if it was his expression or his body language, but I had a sudden flash of inspiration. I knew immediately why I kept thinking I'd met Paul before.

"You," I said, the word escaping my mouth of its own volition.

"Me, what?" he asked moodily.

"You!" I repeated again a little louder, pointing at him.

"Yes, me. I'm Paul, and you're Riley, remember? You come into the bank with massive amounts of pennies, just to make my life difficult."

My mind was working, but I couldn't process the information into speech. When I didn't say anything, he cocked his head, looking at me strangely.

"Did you just have a stroke or something?"

"Where do you live?" I demanded.

"I'm not sure I should tell you, the way you're acting."

"Just tell me where you live."

"I live at the Coventry Apartments. Satisfied?"

"You're the guy—the one I saw attacking his car with a rose bouquet in my parking lot on Valentine's Day!" I gasped.

The color drained from his face and he looked away, clearly embarrassed.

"Well, I guess they don't *all* fall at your feet in admiration, do they?"

His face registered actual pain at that remark, and I was instantly sorry. I knew I went over the line, but it was too late. The cold mask had already fallen back into place, his expression made of stone.

"Paul," I started.

"No, I think we've both had enough for one day. I'm quite busy, and I'm sure there's somewhere you need to be as well."

I looked up at him sadly as I picked up my money.

"You know, if I had shown up at your counter with a deposit slip instead of a bag of pennies, we might have been friends." I turned and walked out the door, wondering what exactly just happened.

. . . .

After the bank, I went back to the office. I slammed drawers and flung papers around, stomping as petulantly as I dared.

"How did it go at the bank?" Sarah finally asked.

"You know. Why does life have to be so complicated? You should either click with a person or not. The whole idea of being really horrible one day, then considerate the next is just too confusing. I think people should just pick one and stick with it, don't you?" I demanded.

"I'm guessing that by 'people,' you mean Paul."

"I don't know what to think. I mean, one day he's a complete jerk, and the next, he's trying to be all understanding."

"So which was it today?"

I rolled my eyes. "Actually, today it was me that was the jerk. And I'm not normally like that! He just has this way of bringing out my nasty side."

"I wasn't aware that you had a nasty side," Sarah commented, an amused look on her face. She was standing on her tiptoes, but she still couldn't get the chart she was reaching for. I got up and handed it to her effortlessly. When I thought back to what I said to Paul, I felt horrible.

Sarah leaned back in her chair, folding her arms across her chest. "Well, you might as well confess. It will make you feel better."

"Some days I swear you can read my mind," I said, sighing loudly. "Paul was so sweet to me the last time I went to the bank that I decided to make him some cookies. . ."

"That's nice . . ."

". . . but when I got there, he was flirting with this blonde, starving model-type, right in front of me!"

"That's not nice."

"Okay, maybe not right in front of me. I was hiding around the corner watching them. But still!"

"So, then what happened?"

"I felt silly about the cookies, so I threw them away."

"Riley, have I taught you nothing? You never throw cookies away, especially not homemade cookies! You should have brought them back here!"

"I was all flustered. I wasn't thinking about the cookies."

"What kind of cookies were they?"

"Forget about the cookies! They're not important. I shouldn't have even mentioned them."

"Okay, then what?"

"Paul was okay, but he mentioned that he saw me spying on him around the corner. He's so cocky sometimes. It was like he was laughing at how silly I was, so I got angry. I asked him if he was only interested in gorgeous, brainless blonde girls, and he accused me of thinking I was better than her!"

"Uh-oh, big mistake."

"So while he was counting out my money, it suddenly came to me in a flash. I knew why I thought he looked familiar. Remember when I told you about that psycho guy in my parking lot on Valentine's Day?"

"That was Paul? Imagine him living in your apartment complex the whole time."

"Yes! And then I made a terrible comment about how obviously, not every woman was falling at his feet. The minute I said it, I wished I could take it back. I think I really hurt him, Sarah—you should have seen his face."

"Yeah, but it sounds like he was egging you on."

"I still shouldn't have said it," I said, hiding my head in my hands. "What am I going to do?"

"Well, as I see it, you have two options. One, you get a new bank and a new apartment and hope that you never see Paul again. Or two, you can go back to the bank and apologize. If he's a decent guy, he'll forgive you, and if he doesn't, you can leave with a clear conscience, knowing that you were the bigger person."

"I don't know. I really don't want to move, but I'm not sure I can face him either. I guess I'll have to think about it."

"That sounds like a good plan. And while you're thinking about it, why don't you walk over to the snack bar and get me a cookie?" Sarah said sweetly.

chapter 11

As the purse is emptied, the heart is filled.

—Victor Hugo

had a hard time falling asleep the night before the fundraiser. It was like I was a little girl again, trying to sleep on Christmas Eve. I was filled with equal parts of anticipation and worry, just praying that everything would go well. Even after I finally did drift off, I kept waking up, afraid that I'd overslept. I was so relieved when the alarm finally went off that I practically jumped out of bed. Whatever happened, good or bad, at least it was finally here.

I arrived at the hospital at about 10:00 to discover that a long white tented area was set up in the courtyard, with signs announcing that the proceeds from our ice cream sales would go to the Riley Madsen Cancer Research Fund. I had to pinch myself to make sure that I was actually awake. I noticed Paula tying bunches of balloons to the surrounding trees, and she waved me over. Today she was wearing large, sparkly purple earrings shaped like thunderbolts. The rest of her clothing seemed quite normal, even dowdy—she just had very odd taste in earrings.

"Paula, this looks incredible, but I've got knots in my stomach. What if no one comes?"

"People will come; you just wait and see. Are you on your way to work?"

"Nope—I'm here to help. I wouldn't miss this for anything."

"Well, they're almost ready to set up the tables, and then we'll start bringing out the ice cream. We've got some coolers, but we're just going to bring out a few kinds at a time so they don't get too melted. Hopefully the customers will start showing up at about 11:00."

I felt excited and sick at the same time. "Just tell me what I can do, and I'll make myself useful."

"They have some white plastic buckets over in Maintenance. I thought we could use a few to collect the money. You could go pick them up."

"Great," I said, eager to feel like I had some purpose other than standing around and getting in the way.

When I returned with my stack of buckets, the tables were out and covered with butcher paper. I deposited the buckets at the end of the tables. I saw Paula with several other people, carrying out tubs of ice cream.

"Riley, I thought you could supervise the money—is that okay?" she said, grunting as she wedged the ice cream carton into the cooler.

"Sure, I'll do whatever you want." I sat in a metal folding chair at the end of the tables near the buckets, feeling a little superfluous. Maybe I should have just gone to work instead. They really had everything under control without me.

People started filtering in slowly as soon as we pried the lids from the first cartons. Several brought whole envelopes or cups full of change, which I knew was more than the price of a cone. We didn't really bother counting the change. The honor system seemed a safe bet at a charity fund-raiser.

I was surprised how many people from the hospital knew who I was, since I didn't recognize many of them. I noticed that the ice cream reduced nearly everyone to at least half their age. They were all smiling and excited. At one point, there were more than thirty people in line, but none of them looked impatient or angry. They all chatted with each other, like kids who are overjoyed when an unexpected fire drill frees them from school temporarily.

Lauren stopped by on her lunch for a scoop of strawberry cheesecake.

"I can't stay very long; three people called in sick today. They weren't going to let me leave at all, but I told them that my best friend organized a full-fledged event, and I had to show my support."

"I didn't organize it; I only had the idea. Plenty of people deserve more credit for this than me."

"It looks like it's going pretty well."

"I know. The line's been like this all morning. It's better than I could have hoped."

"I can't believe that you were responsible for this," she said, looking around in awe while nibbling at her ice cream. "You know, most people want to do something to make a difference but never get around to it. You've actually done it. I'm so impressed."

"Stop it! You're going to make me cry," I threatened.

"Sorry. Stewart proposed again yesterday," she said, quickly changing the subject.

"How'd he do it this time?"

"Hot air balloon."

"You're kidding."

"Do you actually think I could make something like that up?"

"I'm glad it was you and not me. You know how I am with heights; I'd have a heart attack! What did you say?"

"I said no, but every time, it's getting a little harder to turn him down," she said wistfully. "Now I'm going to cry! I'd better get back to work."

I hugged her. "I'm really glad you came."

"I'll call you later and you can give me the report."

My family showed up about 2:00. I felt really proud seeing them all standing together at the back of the line and waving. Mitch held up the line for what seemed like ten minutes, trying to decide what kind of ice cream he wanted. Paula laughed out loud when he finally pointed to the vanilla and said, "I guess I'm just in a vanilla mood today."

I told Mitch to just dump his pennies in the bucket, but he insisted that he had to count them first. He dropped them into the bucket one at a time, panicking when he discovered that he only had ninety-eight. He pulled his pockets inside out but still couldn't discover the two missing pennies. I had some change in my pocket, so I dropped two pennies into his hand. I've never seen anyone look so relieved.

My dad couldn't believe the buckets that were quickly starting to fill up with money. "You've really had quite a turnout today, sweetie," he said, scratching his head.

I felt my face getting hot. "Dad, it wasn't just me. Lots of people worked together to make today happen." But you know how parents are—they can't really be objective about anything where their children are concerned. One of the nicest things about my parents is they are more inclined to believe good things about me than I am myself. They hung around for a while, munching their cones. When they left, my mom made me promise to call her and let her know how much money we raised.

Paula, who had been scooping ice cream for several hours, wandered down to the money collecting end of the operation. "My arm is killing me! Would you like to trade for a while?"

I had secretly wanted to make cones from the start, but I decided to just go with the flow. So when she handed me the metal scoop, I jumped at the chance. I cleaned my hands with a disinfectant wipe and planted myself in front of the pralines and cream. It was a hot day, and even though we were shaded by the tent, I was sweating and my clothes felt sticky. It was difficult to get the first scoops out at the top of the barrel, but as the sun softened the ice cream, the scoop began to slide in more easily.

After the pralines and cream was gone, I started on a tub of Oreo. I was so involved with the scooping and visiting that before I knew it, that tub was gone as well and, even more surprisingly, there was still a line. It went on like that the rest of the afternoon, with lulls and sudden rushes. There was a definite increase in business around 3:30, which made me laugh because that's about the time I start looking for something sweet to get me through the rest of the day.

The next flavor I served was mocha almond, then orange

dreamsicle. Taking the lids off of the cartons was like rediscovering old friends, and I wanted to try every kind.

The girls from my office came in shifts, from the time we opened until about 4:30. They bought so much ice cream that I wondered who could possibly be eating it all. I scooped their ice cream into cups instead of cones so it would be easier to transfer. The second time I saw Sarah appear with the tray, I said, "I have to ask—where is all the ice cream going?"

"Well, we're eating it."

"*All* of it?" I asked incredulously.

"No, the patients are eating some too. Honestly, I feel more like a waitress than a nurse today. How's it going?" she asked, craning her neck toward the buckets of money.

"There have been more people here than I ever imagined. I don't know where they're all coming from—certainly they can't all work here."

"I think sometimes we forget what a big place the hospital really is. Tucked away in our little office, it's easy to forget that there are so many other things going on."

"I guess so. Some of these people have been here twice today. I'm not sure if they have big hearts or just really like ice cream."

"Well, some of us have to get back to work. Stop by on your way out and tell us what the grand total is."

"I'm not sure how long it will take to count it, but I'll try." My eyes followed Sarah as she walked down to pay for her ice cream, oblivious to the fact that there was someone in front of me, waiting. He cleared his throat impatiently. Embarrassed, I began scooping frantically, not bothering to look up to see who it was.

"You know, it's the funniest thing. You look so familiar, but I just can't place you." When I heard that voice, I stopped scooping and looked up into Paul's waiting eyes. I decided to play along.

"Maybe you've seen me around the hospital. I scoop a mean Neapolitan."

"I don't think that's it. My name is Paul, by the way. I didn't catch yours . . . "

"Well, that's because I didn't give it."

He mockingly grabbed his chest over his heart, as if I'd wounded him.

"It's Riley. Riley Madsen," I said, sticking out my sticky ice cream hand for Paul to shake.

"Riley Madsen, I think this is quite the event you've got going here."

"It's not my event. I'm just a menial laborer."

"That's not what I heard."

I gave him a questioning look.

"Kimberly at the bank told me about the pennies and your project. And I saw your name on a poster as I walked up."

"Oh." There was an awkward pause, and I could see that the line was starting to back up behind him. "Neapolitan or cherry chocolate?" I asked briskly.

"I'm really more of an Oreo guy, myself."

"Well, you should have come earlier then. What's it gonna be?"

"Cherry chocolate," he said finally.

I sunk the metal scoop into the ice cream, telling myself not to hope that Paul had an ulterior motive for his visit. I made sure that he got an extra large scoop and handed him the sugar cone almost shyly. He handed me a twenty-dollar bill.

I sighed. "Paul, you work in a bank. Is this really the best change you could come up with?"

He licked his cone innocently. "Is that too much?"

"Very funny. Take it to the end of the line. I'm sure they can work something out."

He pressed it back into my palm. "I told you, I don't need any change. As far as I'm concerned, it still came cheap. I talked to you for five minutes, and we didn't exchange one nasty word."

I hesitated. "Enjoy your ice cream," I whispered, drowning in his beautiful eyes.

He smiled at me. "Bye, Riley."

I was dazed as I walked to turn in the twenty dollars. It was folded in half, and I unfolded it to smooth it out. Inside was a yellow sticky note that read, "Have dinner with me on Saturday?" with his phone number at the bottom.

See, it's true—ice cream makes everyone sweeter.

. . . .

After about 5:00, we were almost completely out of ice cream. I scraped the last of the rocky road into a cone, which I nibbled on as we started to count the money. Fortunately for us, most people don't walk around with hundreds of pennies in their pockets, and most of the proceeds were in bills. But there was still plenty of change in the buckets to sort through. We were shocked to discover that we raised a little over seven hundred dollars. I gaped when Paula announced the final total. That number was so far above any expectations I had that I couldn't find any words to comment.

Several of the people who helped out thanked me for giving them the opportunity to participate. Everyone was glowing with pride over what we'd accomplished. We sat under the trees, enjoying the shade as we finished off the last of the ice cream.

. . . .

I stopped in the office on my way out to share the good news. As I rounded the corner, I heard someone hiss, "There she is!" and a general scurrying commenced.

"What's going on?" I noticed a large poster on my chair, which Sarah grabbed and held over her head. Stacey, Kate, and Celeste popped out from behind me, covering me in handfuls of confetti. The poster screamed, "Congratulations, Riley!" in large, bright lettering.

"What is this?"

"We're just proud of you, that's all. You did a really good thing today," Kate said, throwing a little more confetti for good measure.

"Okay, enough with the praise. What we really want to know is, how much money did you make?" Sarah asked impatiently.

"$709.32," I answered happily.

"That is absolutely amazing," Stacey breathed in awe. Everyone nodded.

"So what are you going to do to top this, Riley?" Celeste asked.

I hadn't even considered it. I was still reeling from the day's success. What *was* I going to do?

. . . .

I walked to my car, breathing in the loveliness of late summer and basking in the warmth. I noticed in dismay that I'd left the window cracked a few inches that morning. Brilliant, Riley—it's a good thing it didn't rain.

As I got closer to the car, I could see that there was something shiny on my front seat. I peered into the car, surprised to see my driver's seat and floor covered with a layer of pennies; it was like a tiny money storm in my car. I opened the door carefully so none would escape, wondering how I was going to drive home. I found a plastic grocery bag in my back seat and started shoveling in the change. I uncovered a folded slip of pink paper under the sheet of pennies on the seat. It read, "Just a small contribution to your fund."

It was unsigned, except for the words, "Someone Who Sees."

The smell of autumn was heavy, carried on the cool breeze like a song, the words in a forgotten ancient language. I took a deep breath, enjoying the heady aroma of the dried leaves. I set the stack of cardboard boxes I was carrying on the lawn and crouched down to begin my treasured chore.

Every year when the massive tree in the front yard dropped its load of black walnuts onto my grandparents' lawn, our family helped gather them up in boxes. When Grandpa was alive, he loved to carve the shells into faces with his pocketknife. Some were friendly looking, while others glared at you like angry demons.

Now, with only Grandma left, it would be nearly impossible for her to gather the harvest alone. Fortunately, it was a task our family relished. We raked the leaves into a wheelbarrow, and Mom and Dad took turns giving the younger kids a ride. They sat perched on top of the crunchy leaves, the current king or queen until they reached the garden, where the leaves were deposited and someone else demanded their turn. After the work was done, Grandma gathered us inside for hot chocolate and homemade caramel popcorn balls.

That year, my mom and dad were worried because the family was going on vacation in the fall, all except for me. I had to stay behind because I was starting college and didn't want to miss my first week of school. But I assured them that I would be happy to take on the task of cleaning up the yard by myself this time. Grandma told me to put on gloves so the walnuts wouldn't stain my fingers. I told her I didn't mind—it was my favorite part. I liked the pungent green smell that clung to my hands and clothing long after the task was finished. It reminded me of Grandpa.

I filled one box easily, carrying it to the garage and depositing it *near the front. I saw no reason to go in any farther than was absolutely necessary. As long as I didn't disturb the cobwebby darkness, I hoped the spiders would show me the same courtesy.*

When I returned to start filling the next box, I noticed a man wearing a backpack, sitting at the bus stop bench in front of the house. His clothing was expensive, and he wore it well, as if he were fully aware of how good-looking he was. His green eyes glinted in the sunlight, and he watched me with amusement.

"What have you got to smile about?" he asked, his voice lazy but confident.

I stood up, brushing the dirt from the knees of my jeans. "I'm enjoying myself."

"What is there to enjoy? It looks like a nasty chore to me."

"You wouldn't understand."

"Try me."

"It reminds me of being a kid."

"I always had to mow the lawn when I was a kid. I hated it."

I laughed. "See what I mean? You wouldn't understand."

He returned my laugh. "I guess you're right. I'm Brian, by the way," he said, extending his hand for me to shake.

I stood for a minute, pretending to consider. "My grandmother always told me to watch out for the weirdos waiting for the bus, but you look safe enough. I'm Riley."

"Nice to meet you, Riley." When he released my hand, he noticed in dismay that his was now covered in sticky black walnut grunge. He brushed it off on his pant leg.

"So, where are you going on the bus?"

"To class."

"You're a student?"

"I'm just starting my senior year," he said importantly.

"Really? My classes start tomorrow afternoon, but I'm only a lowly freshman."

"Imagine that. Maybe I could show you around."

"Actually, that would be nice. I'm forever getting lost, and I don't see how I'm going to pass my classes if I can't even find them. Maybe we could meet here and ride the bus together," I said hopefully.

He laughed as the bus lumbered up to the stop, the brakes announcing its arrival with a shriek. "Oh, I don't ride the bus," he said, waiting for the door to open.

"You could have fooled me."

He ran up the steps, turning to bend down in the doorway. "My car's in the shop. I'll pick you up here tomorrow at noon."

Before I could reply, the doors closed and the bus jerked ahead clumsily. Brian waved to me from his window.

chapter 12

When you do the common things in life in an uncommon way, you will command the attention of the world.

—George Washington Carver

I woke up on Saturday morning to discover that I was famished. I hadn't done anything different than usual the night before. I ate dinner, just like I always do. But that morning, my stomach felt completely hollowed out. I pulled my hair back in clips and threw on some clothes. It was unusually cool outside, and I almost wished I'd grabbed a jacket as I walked to the bagel place a couple of blocks from my apartment.

By the time I got there, my stomach was protesting that it must have been days since it last saw food. Before I knew what I was doing, I had consumed two huge chocolate chip bagels slathered in cream cheese at record-breaking speed. I chased that down with a big glass of orange juice, finally starting to feel full. It was about then that I remembered that I was going out with Paul that night.

It was nerves—that's why I was so hungry. Most people can't eat when they're anxious about something, but not me. I eat twice as much as usual, just to have something to focus on other than the latest impending catastrophe. The bagels sank to the bottom of my stomach like a rock. I only hoped I would still be able to zip up my jeans that night.

. . . .

I was more tense getting ready to go out with Paul than any other date in recent memory, probably because most of them were blind dates. Maybe I was sabotaging myself, but with a blind date, it's always there in the back of my mind that if this guy doesn't work out, there's bound to be another one. You have no expectations. But with Paul, it was different. Something told me that this was our last chance to at least be friends.

I knew from experience that he had the capability of being quite cruel when provoked, but I had also witnessed him being kinder than any guy I knew. If only I could train myself to bring out his good side instead of the bad. I'm not sure what it was about me that tended to bring out the worst in Paul, but if I had to bite my tongue until it bled, I was prepared to do it. Even if we didn't exactly click romantically, we just had to be friends.

I purposely chose a shirt without buttons, because my hands were shaking so much I was sure it would take me half an hour just to deal with them. It was my favorite brown shirt. Dark colors are slimming, and after the bagel incident that morning, I needed all the help I could get.

I kept thinking about the woman who must have inspired the Valentine's Day massacre in the parking lot. Perhaps Paul had a good reason I knew nothing about for being bitter about relationships. Thinking of him as damaged made him even more attractive somehow. Maybe I should consider therapy.

I was still mulling over the strange penny delivery I found in my car after the fund-raiser. Every time I thought about it, I couldn't help smiling. I hadn't told anyone about it yet, not even Lauren. It was kind of nice having a secret. I don't know why, but I was sure it was a guy who left them. The handwriting looked masculine, and the pink paper suggested a secret admirer, but I didn't want to get my hopes up. I pictured the Penny Guy (which was what I started calling him) showing up on his white horse, scooping me up, and galloping off into the sunset. As I said before, I'm terrified of horses, but in that situation, I think I could make an exception.

I knew it was a long shot, but it didn't hurt to dream. Who could he be? Maybe he was a guy from work who was shy and couldn't confront me in person. He could be *the one*. Can you imagine having that as the story of how you met? It's perfect, almost as good as mine and Paul's, or Lauren's and Stewart's.

The doorbell rang, snapping me back from my little daydream. I squared my shoulders and hurried to the door, opening it expectantly. Paul flashed me a smile, looking hot in a black shirt and jeans.

"Right on time. But then, I guess that's one of the perks of living in the same apartment complex as your date," I said, locking the door behind me.

As we made our way to his car, I noticed that he was sneaking glances at me when he thought I wasn't looking. "What?" I finally asked.

"I didn't say anything." He opened my door, and I slid in. I waited for him to open his door on the other side.

"I know you didn't say anything, but you've been looking at me really weird," I told him.

"Was I? I didn't realize." His eyes involuntarily gave me the once-over before he turned to put the key in the ignition.

"You just did it again!"

He started laughing, and I suddenly felt like I was in one of those dreams where you realize that you're in a public place with no clothes on.

"If you don't tell me what's going on, this is going to be the shortest date ever," I threatened.

"It's nothing, really. I just realized that this is the first time I've ever seen you with real clothes on."

It took me a minute to figure out what he was talking about. "Oh, you mean the scrubs. I do own normal clothes, you know."

"I can see that. It's just like, I don't know . . . running into your doctor at the grocery store."

"Thanks a lot."

"It just never occurred to me, okay?"

"I can go back in and put my scrubs on if you want," I said, putting my hand on the car door handle.

"Don't be silly. You look . . . nice."

"I'm going to take that as a compliment and move on."

He cleared his throat. "I thought we could have Chinese for dinner, unless you're not a fan, and maybe a movie after?"

"Sounds great."

As he pulled out of the parking lot, I said, "Just for the record, I've never seen you in real clothes either. I think I'm handling it pretty well."

. . . .

Dinner was actually a lot of fun. I really like Chinese food, and Paul was quite impressed when he saw how adept I am with chopsticks. He fumbled with them for a while before opting for a fork. Our conversation was lively but not in the least heated. We sailed through the sesame chicken and noodles with barely a raised voice. He told me about his family, who live out of state. He has one younger brother in college who he misses a lot. His eyes were laughing as he told me a story about the two of them sinking a canoe at camp one summer.

I filled him in on my family as well. He couldn't believe I had so many siblings. I regaled him with some of my stories about Mitch, who is always good for comic relief. As I talked, I watched Paul's face. He was so calm, relaxed, and unguarded. I couldn't believe how well things were going.

Just when I thought the night couldn't get any better, I noticed that Paul's grin had suddenly turned into an expression of uneasy hesitation, like there was something he was dreading. I couldn't understand what had happened. I picked at the leftover noodles until I couldn't stand the suspense any longer.

"Paul, did I say something wrong?" I blurted out.

"Why would you say that?"

"You just got quiet in the last five minutes, and I thought something might be bothering you."

"Actually, there is something I have to tell you, and I feel really guilty about it."

"You're not married, are you?"

He laughed out loud. "Of course not! I'm not that kind of guy."

"You just seemed so serious, and you having a wife at home was the worst scenario I could think of."

"No, it's about when we met." He hesitated. "The first time I saw you in the bank, well, the first couple of times, I had just gotten out of a serious relationship. It ended on Valentine's Day, which you so ably reminded me."

"I didn't realize you were the same guy at first, and then it just clicked. Paul, I had no right to say what I did about you. It was unspeakably rude. I felt really bad about how I behaved. I was so glad you showed up at the fund-raiser, because I knew you wouldn't bother to come if you hated me."

"It wasn't your fault. I provoked you, and you struck back. Anyway, what I wanted to say was the first time I met you, you were happy and friendly, and I was just angry with the whole world. I was in a bad place, and I took it out on you. I'm really sorry, Riley, and I'm glad you decided to give me a second chance."

I was speechless. When I finally recovered my voice, I raised my water glass. "Here's to second chances." Paul looked relieved and smiled as our glasses clinked.

By the time they brought the fortune cookies, we were laughing and joking again like old friends. I loved hearing his laugh, and even more, I liked being able to make him laugh. I gaped when I cracked open my cookie, which read, "Your temper is legendary, but you have a good heart."

"Did you plant this?" I asked, feigning insult but secretly pleased.

"Why? What does it say?"

I handed it across the table so he could read it. "No," he said, snickering. "I wish I'd thought of it—it certainly is true enough."

"All right then, Mr. Smug, what does yours say?" I folded my arms across my chest and leaned back into the cushy booth.

He opened his cookie and frowned. "I'm sure you didn't plant this one."

"How could I? I didn't even know we were coming here. Come on, I read you mine."

"It says, 'Stay away from women in the medical profession.' "

My mouth dropped open. "It does not! Fortune cookies don't say things like that!" I tried to grab it, but he crumpled it up and hid it under his plate.

"I don't think we should come here anymore," he said. "I won't allow you to be insulted by strange cookies like that."

"How very gallant of you."

Paul paid the check, and we got up to leave. When he wasn't looking, I retrieved his mangled fortune and stuffed it into my pocket.

. . . .

With the exception of Paul's mystery fortune, everything was going beautifully until about halfway through the movie. Paul bought a bucket of popcorn, even though we'd only finished dinner an hour ago. Which was fine with me. I'm one of those people who thinks that the movie experience isn't complete without popcorn—the greasier, the better. My pants were getting dangerously tight, but I would deal with the consequences later.

As I grabbed aimless handfuls of popcorn, I tried to sneak quick peeks at Paul. His face looked quite striking in the glow from the screen, and although our fingers did meet occasionally in the shared bucket, he made no attempts to grasp anything other than popcorn. I sighed, turning my attention back to the movie.

I suddenly became aware of something inching its way up my arm. This would have been a welcome development, had it turned out to be Paul. Instead, I was confronted with a medium-sized, hairy spider. And by medium-sized, I mean he was approximately the size of a compact car instead of an SUV. Before I could stop myself, I shrieked in a there's-a-serial-killer-chasing-me-with-a-knife fashion. I smacked the popcorn as I flailed my arms around, trying to get rid of my little unwanted companion. The bucket hit the ground, kernels jumping out in all directions.

I am deathly afraid of spiders, which you've probably guessed by now. To put it into perspective, I would rather water ski naked on a frozen lake than come face-to-face with your average spider. I don't know which was worse: the idea that the spider came in with me, a silent inhabitant of my person, or that he came as a complimentary gift with the popcorn, just lurking in the buttery darkness.

The spider was no longer on my arm, which presented an issue nearly as pressing—that of Disappearing Spider. It was here, then it wasn't. *Where was it?*

I looked at Paul, who was staring at me like I'd just taken a meat cleaver out of my purse and started casually sharpening it. I located the spider making its way toward my shoe, and I froze. Not even if my life depended on it could I muster the courage to squash the spider with my shoe. Besides, these were new shoes. Even if I did suddenly grow a backbone and stomp on the spider, I'd have to throw them away. All I could do was point at it wildly and hyperventilate as it crept ever closer to my foot. Soon, it would crawl up my leg, I would have a stroke, and the next thing you know, the nurses are passing around my obituary at work.

Paul gave me a "you've got to be kidding me" look, calmly stpped on the spider, and tried to ignore the looks the entire theater was giving us. Now that the crisis had passed, I shrunk back into my seat, feeling even smaller than what was left of the spider on the floor. When Paul finally looked at me again, I leaned over and whispered, "I don't much care for spiders."

He stared in disbelief for a minute, then started to laugh in that silent way where no noise comes out and you can't breathe. When he could finally talk again, he said, "I think I was more scared than you were. I was so relieved when I saw the spider. I thought you were having some sort of epileptic fit!"

I laughed until my face hurt and tried not to focus on the nasty looks we were getting from everyone else.

· · · · · · · · · · ·

When Paul dropped me off at the door, we were still joking about the spider fiasco.

"You really know how to keep your head in a crisis. Most of the time I have to pay someone for spider disposal services," I joked.

"Well, thank you, Riley, for a most interesting and entertaining evening."

We both stood silently for a moment, not moving. It finally became too awkward for me, and I opened my arms for a hug. I never know how long you're supposed to hug someone on a first date. I've often wished there was a timer. When the bell rings, you separate and go to your corners. It's the same with kissing, I suppose, but that's really never been an issue for me. Our hug was the shortest possible, with Paul pulling away quickly.

"Good night, Riley," he said, practically running to his car.

I unlocked the door and went in, closing it behind me. Well, that was that. The stupid spider had ruined my chances with Paul, since he obviously thought I was crazy now. Why did these things always have to happen to me? I tried not to give in to the tears I felt burning the corners of my eyes. When I took off my jeans to put on my pajamas, I stumbled onto Paul's forgotten fortune: "Your soul mate is closer than you think."

chapter 13

Most people would rather be certain they're miserable, than risk being happy.

—Robert Anthony

On Monday everyone was dying to know about my date, and since I am a rotten liar, I told them the whole, terrible truth. I'd been hoping that no one would bring it up, but they all knew how excited I was. So of course, the nurses wasted no time in pouncing on me the minute I walked through the door. Since I'd been rehearsing it all day Sunday, I managed to get through the story and even laugh a little along with them. I left out the part about Paul's fortune, just as I didn't tell anyone about my potential admirer. I was getting to be a woman of mystery, and I liked the fact that there were things about me that no one knew.

I got home from work on Wednesday night, determined to be lazy. I was just sitting down to a microwave rice bowl and a *Friends* rerun when the doorbell rang. My doorbell actually ringing is such a rare occurrence that sometimes I ring it myself, just to make sure it still works. I get about the same number of people showing up at my door as the number of calls on my cell phone. It's one of those necessary items, but when only my mother, Lauren, or one of my sisters ever call it, I have a hard time justifying the expense.

When I opened the door, there was a flower delivery guy standing there with the most beautiful dozen red roses I'd ever seen. The smell wafted in the door before he even had a chance to say anything.

"I'm sorry, you're probably looking for next door," I said, starting to close the door.

"Are you Riley Madsen?" he asked, sniffling.

"Yes . . . ?"

"Sign here, please," he said, pointing at a line on his clipboard, sniffling again. His eyes and nose were red, and he seemed to be sniffing a lot. Maybe he was allergic to flowers. Can you imagine how ridiculous that would be? It's like being an exterminator with a bug phobia. But maybe that would be liberating, in a way. Or he could have been on drugs. Either way, he looked miserable, and I felt sorry for him. I initialed the paper on the clipboard, trading his pen for the gorgeous bouquet. It seemed awfully heavy for flowers, but then, it had been a long time. Perhaps I'd forgotten.

I figured the flowers must be from Paul, which was confusing to say the least, considering how we parted. I don't know anyone else who would send me flowers, except maybe my mother, and it wasn't my birthday.

"You'd better get those in water right away," the delivery guy said helpfully.

I studied the vase, which was made of creamy white milk glass. Okay, so he definitely was on drugs. What did he think they were in now—Jell-O? But when I examined it closer, I could see that the flower stems were carefully nestled in pennies.

"What's with the pennies anyway?" he asked.

"It's a long story," I said, distractedly searching out the card. I found the little white envelope with "Riley" on the front. I didn't recognize the handwriting. Instead of a card, inside was a folded piece of pink paper that read:

> Roses are red,
> Your eyes are soft blue,
> I hear you like pennies—
> I've left some for you.
> In case you are stumped
> And you want to know more,
> It was me who left pennies
> Inside your car door.

The delivery guy sniffed again. I'd forgotten he was still there.

"Thanks a lot," I said, closing the door. He looked a little disappointed. I think he expected me to read him the card.

Well, I guess this made it official. This definitely fit under the secret admirer category. I took the roses to the kitchen table, where I carefully emptied out the pennies into a plastic bag. I filled the vase with water, leaving it in the center of the table where I could admire the flowers. I kept coming up with reasons to go back into the kitchen for the rest of the night so I could look at them. I finally gave up and just sat down at the table.

This guy was proving to be a distraction. No one had done anything half as romantic for me in ages, and it stirred something in me that I had forgotten existed.

I'm not sad that I'm not married, but I wouldn't complain if someone paid a little attention every now and then. Well, there was Paul, *was* being the operative word. He was the closest I'd come lately to anything resembling a relationship. I wasn't quite to the point yet where I could see the humor in our tragic date, but there was definite potential. Wait until I told my sisters about that date! That would teach Olivia that it wasn't all first kisses and candlelight dinners.

I guess the last time I got roses like these was years ago from my fiancé, Brian. No, you didn't fall asleep and miss a chapter. I had a fiancé once. It seems such a long time ago now, and in another lifetime altogether. But there was someone once. I've pushed him out of my mind so completely that it's hard for me to recall him now. Oh, I remember his name and things about him. But I no longer remember the exact shade of his eyes. I can't remember now the way it felt to hold his hand when we went for a walk on a crisp autumn evening. He was, for me, *the one*, as Lauren would say. But there was only one problem—I wasn't *the one* for him.

There, I've said it. Not every love story ends with happily ever after; mine certainly didn't. Sometimes the prince has his eye on another princess, and you're so busy trying to decide how to decorate the castle that you don't even notice. Suddenly, you're left in the lurch, wondering where it all went wrong.

You can understand now where the control issues come from.

So why bother putting your heart out there when it's just going to get stomped on? Why show the best bits of yourself to anyone, when it only opens you up to getting hurt again? Maybe Lauren is right—live your own life, and wait for your prince to come to you.

The flowers were lovely, but were they really worth it?

. . . .

The ringing telephone brought me out of my pity fest. I considered not answering it, continuing my barefoot walk through the glass shards of memory lane. But it could be my mother, and I suddenly wanted very much to hear a friendly voice. At this point, I'd even settle for Mitch.

"Hello?"

"Hi, Riley." Long pause. "It's Paul. Did I catch you at a bad time?"

What did he want? Gloating is really such a juvenile quality. "No, I'm just . . . hanging out."

Smooth. Really smooth. "You?"

"Um . . . me too. Hanging out."

Obviously, if this relationship had started over the phone, it wouldn't have lasted five minutes.

"I was just calling to see if you wanted to go out again this weekend."

You have got to be kidding me.

"Riley?"

"Oh, I'm here. I'm just trying to process it. Tell me, do you enjoy embarrassing public displays?"

"Not exactly."

"Then you must love awkward scenes at the doorstep."

"Nope."

"Well then, that settles it. It's the spider killing. You must really crave the spider killing."

"Absolutely. Never miss a chance."

"You know, I was positive you'd never look at me again, after that whole humiliating incident in the theater."

"Oh no—I thought you showed true courage and . . . bravery."

"Right. So, if I didn't scare you off, why did you run away so fast? You hugged me like I had leprosy."

He cleared his throat. "Well, to be honest, you looked so cute doing that whole spider dance earlier, I was afraid that if I stuck around, I wouldn't be able to stop myself from kissing you. And you don't seem like the kiss-on-the-first-date type. So I fled."

The room temperature on my side of the phone went up at least ten degrees instantly. "I don't usually kiss on the first date. But, for the knight in shining armor that vanquished the evil, fire-breathing spider, I might have made an exception. But I guess we'll never know now, will we?"

I actually think I heard Paul gulp on the other end of the line.

"What do you think the chances are of finding another spider in the same theater?" he mused.

"Probably not great."

"I guess not. I don't suppose you know any really dirty restaurants with lots of code violations?"

"Uh, no."

"Oh well, I'll figure something out. How about Friday?"

"Really? Are you sure you want to do that?"

"I double-dog dare you to go out with me again. Is that clear enough for you?"

"Well, you're in for it then, because I never turn down a challenge."

"Friday at 7:00, then. Bye, Riley."

Hmmm. Maybe it is worth it.

. . . .

The minute I hung up with Paul, I dialed Lauren's number. I didn't bother to say hello when she picked up.

"Second date, second daaaaaaate," I sang into the phone.

"Aaaaaaahhhh!" she squealed. "See, I knew it—he is smitten with you. Maybe we could have a double wedding, " she said coyly.

I laughed. "Yeah, maybe two or three years down the road, you'll get tired of crushing Stewart's hopes and say yes."

She hesitated. "It might not be that long."

"You finally said yes, didn't you!"

"No. But he did."

I was stunned. "I don't get it. What happened?"

"Well, I'd pretty much made up my mind to say yes the next time he asked. But two whole weeks went by without him asking me, and I thought he might have given up. So I decided to take matters into my own hands."

I couldn't help giggling. "What did you say?"

"I was making dinner for him tonight at my house, and he was watching TV on the couch. So I yelled and asked him if he could come into the kitchen to help me with something. I gave him a bottle of something to open, and when he was done, I said, 'By the way, while you're in here, could you help me with this ring?' "

"And?"

"It took him a minute to figure out what I was asking, and then it was like the light just went on. He had this huge grin on his face as he slid the ring on my finger."

"Lauren, I'm so happy for you!" I gushed.

"And I'm happy for you too—second date!"

"Well, it kind of seems small in comparison to your news."

"I'd better go. Stewart went out to get some sparkling cider to celebrate. He ought to be back any minute."

"Tell him I said congratulations. I'll talk to you tomorrow, soon-to-be married woman."

As I hung up, I felt an overwhelming sense of dread plummeting until it landed in my stomach like a rock.

My best friend was getting married.

I really was happy for her. I'd only met Stewart a few times, but he seemed like a nice guy, and I've always wanted Lauren to meet someone who truly appreciated her.

So why along with the well wishes was there an equal amount of resentment? I wondered for the first time if this was the way Lauren felt when I'd gotten engaged to Brian, but somehow I didn't think she was capable of any mean feelings toward me, and that made me feel even worse.

I convinced myself that it was late, I was tired, and I really should just go to bed and stop feeling sorry for myself. Everything would look better in the morning.

· · · · · · · · · · ·

It is pitch black outside, the middle of the night. I am running into the backyard of the house where I grew up, and although I know we are in the present, it's as if I never left. I have a flashlight and I switch it on, cutting a path through the darkened grass. I also have a shovel, and I can't shake the desperate feeling that I've lost something. I come to a spot that is familiar, and I dig and dig. I dig right through the grass, throwing dirt and rocks all over the lawn. When I become frustrated with my lack of progress in that spot, I move to another and begin tearing up the ground there instead. Clumps of grass are flying all around me as I move from one patch to another. To my dismay, my shovel seems to be shrinking. It gets smaller and smaller until it disappears completely. I drop to my hands and knees, using my fingers to dig through the wet, cold ground. I claw through the dirt until my fingers are bloody, but I still can't find whatever it is I've lost.

I suddenly opened my eyes, finding myself in my apartment, in my own bed. My breath was ragged and the sheets were tangled around me. There was sweat trickling down my back from my struggle. It was only a dream.

I climbed out of bed and padded into the kitchen for a glass of water. I gulped it eagerly, trying to remember what I'd lost. I'd always been really interested in dream interpretation, and I finally decided it must be my subconscious revealing my fear of losing my best friend.

On impulse, I went back into my room and switched on the light in the closet. I had to sift through several boxes before I found what I was looking for. I undid the clasp on my old penny necklace and fastened it around my neck securely. It felt cool against my skin. I switched out the light and went back to bed, falling asleep almost immediately.

. . . .

"So, what about ice cream? Anybody game?" Celeste asked hopefully.

"I'm in," Sarah said, holding a dollar in the air.

"It's butter pecan. Do you even have to ask?" I said happily.

Celeste went into the back to clean up one of the rooms. I said that I would go pick up the ice cream, since everyone else was busy. I took the orders and gathered the money, making my way toward the snack bar. Today they had orange sherbet, chocolate raspberry sundae, Oreo, and butter pecan. My mouth was watering, just thinking about the butter pecan. I almost felt like skipping as I turned the corner into the snack bar.

Paula was there, sporting jingly earrings that brushed her shoulders, and we chatted while she and another woman I didn't know took care of my order.

"Oh, I almost forgot—someone left this for you." Paula handed me a small pink paper, all rolled up with a ribbon tied around it. I snatched it from her hand, sliding off the ribbon to read the note. As I opened it, I could see that the paper was rolled around a dollar bill.

The note said, "They have butter pecan today, so I thought you might be here. This one's on me."

I wasn't sure whether I should be flattered or terrified. I grabbed Paula's shoulders, pulling her toward me. "The man who brought this—did you recognize him?"

She looked a little scared. "I don't think I've ever seen him before. Why, is something wrong?"

I let go of her, and she shrank back, like she'd never seen me before either. "I'm sorry. It's just that, I don't know who he is. He's like a . . . secret admirer or something," I mumbled.

"Oh, Riley, isn't that exciting? Well, now that I think of it, he was quite handsome. I remember thinking he had lovely green eyes."

"Green eyes? Are you sure?" The desperation in my voice crept up a notch.

"Positive. I'll keep an eye out for him, but he wasn't dressed like he works here."

"Thanks, Paula." I gave her the money that I brought with me, tucking the pink note and the dollar into the pocket of my scrubs. Here I was, excited to be going out with Paul again, the first nice guy I've met in forever, and now the Penny Guy shows up to confuse things.

As I walked back to the office, I couldn't help being a little disappointed, which is hard to do carrying a tray of ice cream, believe me. It's just that I was certain that the Penny Guy's eyes were going to be blue.

"C'mon," I said impatiently, dragging him by his arm toward the bakery. "Aren't you excited to pick a cake?"

"I just thought you could choose one by yourself. You don't really need me here. It could be like a surprise! I'm not a huge cake fan anyway. In fact, we could just skip the cake part altogether, set a trend. Who needs a cake?"

I stopped and gave him a dangerous look, my hand resting on the doorknob.

He raised his hands in defeat. "Okay, you win. Let's start picking cakes."

I pulled open the door, and the dense smell of pastry came pouring out, a delicious wave of sugar and eggs. There were books with pictures of any flavor, shape, or color of cake you could imagine. The walls were lined with glass cases, displaying examples of the delicately handcrafted work of the bakers, each seeming more perfect than the last.

"This is heaven," I breathed.

"This isn't going to take all night, is it?" he asked anxiously.

"Brian!" I scolded.

The argument was thwarted when a door in the back opened. A thin blonde woman appeared, her hair pulled back in an elegant twist. She gave us a gracious smile.

"Welcome to Bliss. You must be Riley and . . . ?"

"Brian," he said smoothly, offering her his hand.

"Brian, of course. You'll have to forgive me. This is our busiest time of year, and we've been absolutely swamped. But we're so glad you considered us for something as important as your wedding cake. After all, the cake is one of the most crucial parts of the wedding," she stressed.

"That's what I've been trying to tell him! He wouldn't care if we didn't have a cake at all," I said.

The woman gave me a sympathetic look. "Men. They don't have a clue, do they?" she said, tittering politely. "I'm Lisa, by the way. I'll be helping you choose your cake today. Do you have any ideas about what you'd like?"

I glanced around the room. "To tell you the truth, I'm a little bit overwhelmed. Do you have any suggestions?"

"Actually, we have a selection of some of our most popular cakes for you to try, if you're interested."

"That would be great!" I said enthusiastically.

"I'll be right back," Lisa said. "You two just look around and see if anything catches your eye."

"That's so nice that they actually let you try the cakes. I'm glad we chose this place, aren't you? Honey?"

Brian's eyes were riveted in the direction of the door that Lisa had disappeared behind.

"Earth to Brian!"

He forced himself to look at me, smiling apologetically.

"What happened to you just now? It was like you were a million miles away."

"I was just thinking about how perfect our wedding is going to be: the perfect cake, the perfect flowers, and you, looking stunning in your perfect dress." He gave me a quick peck on the cheek.

"Awww, aren't you sweet? See, I knew you'd come around. This wedding is going to be great. You just wait and see."

Lisa returned and deposited a tray on the table between us. "Feel free to try whichever ones you like."

"Oooh, a dark chocolate cake with white fondant! What a great idea, for a black and white wedding. Do you want to try it, honey?"

"We're not having a black and white wedding, sweetie."

"I know, but you love chocolate cake," I said.

"I'm really full. If I had known we were actually going to be eating cakes instead of just looking at them, I would have saved some room."

I nibbled the chocolate cake, wiping my mouth on a napkin. "Mmmm, delicious." My attention had already wandered back to the tray, trying to decide which bit of pastry to try next.

Lisa came back into the room.

"What flavor is that one?" I asked, pointing to a white cake with intricate frosting designs in pale yellow.

"Lemon buttercream," Lisa answered.

I carefully picked up the wedge. "You sure you don't want any?" I said, offering it to Brian.

"I'm stuffed."

I took a bite, closing my eyes and chewing reverently. "That . . . is amazing," I mumbled.

"There's actually one in the display case, if you'd like to take a look."

I jumped out of my chair, searching the cases eagerly. "I don't see it."

"It's down there—near the end," Lisa said distractedly, never once breaking eye contact with Brian.

I found the cake, studying it carefully from every angle. I wasn't sure I could actually slice into something that fancy. I pictured the knife sliding into it, and myself licking a bit of sugary filling from my fingers before carefully feeding a chunk to my new husband.

Brian picked up the black and white chocolate slice that I had been trying to induce him to sample. He pulled off a little piece and raised it to Lisa's mouth. She ate it quickly.

"I think we have a winner!" I said, clapping my hands excitedly. I noticed Brian holding the slice of chocolate cake with a chunk missing. "I knew you'd give in and try it."

"I couldn't help myself. And you were right . . . it was delicious."

chapter 14

I've had a perfectly wonderful evening. But this wasn't it.

—Groucho Marx

Between the Penny Guy and the office pig, all my spare time lately was pretty much devoted to rolling pennies. This gave me a lot of time to think, but I still didn't have any ideas about what the next big money-making scheme would be, and I was running out of time. I couldn't believe it was the beginning of September already; the year was going by so fast. There was a chill in the air that wasn't there two weeks ago, and I knew that soon the leaves would turn vibrant shades of red, orange, and gold, with winter looming close behind.

The most current total for the fund was $812.37. After the fund-raiser, Paul helped me set up an account in my name where people could donate, if they wanted. I called our local city paper, and they agreed to run a small ad at no charge, telling the public which bank they could go to if they had extra pennies they wanted to contribute. The money wasn't exactly streaming in; it was more like a slow trickle. But I felt more comfortable knowing the money was somewhere safe, and it was earning interest instead of being wedged under my mattress. I also got permission to put out collection jars at the cash registers of several local grocery stores. They had a label on the front explaining what my fund was about and asking people to donate their spare pennies to cancer research. I planned to stop by a couple of times a week to empty them.

It was Friday, and I intended to go to the bank at lunch and deposit the latest round of pennies. I also thought it would be good to see Paul before tonight—sort of break the ice, so it wasn't so weird later. After his comment on the phone about kissing, I think I was probably more nervous now than I was on our first date. If I could just get through the night without being a complete klutz, I think we'd be past the worst of the really awkward phase.

There are some days at work where it seems like people just keep showing up, whether they have an appointment or not. This was proving to be one of those days. I was so busy trying to find spots for our surprise patients and answering the phones that I didn't realize it was past lunch until my stomach told me so. I was shocked to see that it was already 2:00.

I grabbed my car keys and purse, telling Kate that I was running to the bank and I'd be right back. We were busy enough that I probably shouldn't have left, but they'd be okay without me for a few minutes.

My heart thumped crazily in my chest as I walked calmly into the bank with my paper lunch sack full of penny rolls. It beat even faster when I glimpsed Paul at the counter. He was talking to another teller, laughing about something. I walked up to the counter in front of him and plopped the brown bag down. His face brightened a little. Was it possible he was as excited to see me as I was to see him?

"I didn't think I'd be seeing you until later. How sweet of you to bring me lunch."

"Sorry to disappoint you, but it's not exactly peanut butter and jelly," I said, opening the bag so he could peek inside.

"It's all business with you, isn't it? People have to eat, you know. I guess it's a good thing I already ate lunch. I imagine pennies are almost impossible to digest." He paused. "By the way, I was going to call you. Do you think we could push tonight back to tomorrow?"

"That's the most confusing thing I've ever heard."

"You know what I mean. Can we go out tomorrow instead?"

I frowned. "Are you bored with me already?" I teased. "Because if you want to break up, just come right out and say it."

He chuckled. "No, you're already more excitement than I can handle. My brother's been in town for a few days, and he's flying out tonight. I told him I'd drive him to the airport, as long as you don't mind."

"Of course I don't mind. I mean, you hardly ever see him."

"Great! We'll plan on tomorrow then."

"Okay, see you tomorrow." I started toward the door.

"Miss Madsen, I think you're forgetting something . . . "

The bag of pennies was still in my hand. "Right. You were going to take care of these for me, weren't you?" I said, blushing fiercely.

I set the bag down on the counter, but Paul made no immediate move to take it. His eyes were fixed on my neck, and for a minute I was afraid I was dating a closet vampire. I pictured him ringing the doorbell to pick me up for our next date, dressed in a black cape lined with red velvet.

His hand came slowly across the counter, his fingers grazing my neck as he pulled the chain out from where it was hidden beneath my scrubs, revealing the penny at the end.

He leaned in, squinting at it briefly. "A penny. I should have known." He glanced at the bag, then back at the necklace. "What makes that one so special?"

"Well, it's not just any penny," I said quietly. We were almost whispering now, and it struck me as odd that we were having this moment at the bank where Paul worked, with all these other people around. Things like this were supposed to happen during moonlit walks on the beach. The blood rushing through my veins pounded in my ears.

"It looks pretty ordinary to me."

"Maybe you're not looking hard enough," I said, my voice barely audible. I blushed again when I realized how that sounded, and it was obvious we weren't talking about pennies anymore. Paul leaned even closer, and my eyes drifted closed. He's going to kiss me, right in the middle of the bank. My brain screamed for me to put a stop to this, but it was like trying to stop a train wreck after the train has already derailed. My breath froze in my throat as I waited, but nothing happened. I opened my eyes to see Paul, his face deathly pale. There was a man standing at the window next to me wearing a ski mask, and he was pointing a gun at the other teller.

. . . .

There weren't very many people in the bank, but it didn't take them long to figure out what was happening. In fact, I think I was the last one to know, I had been so caught up in the spell Paul was casting.

"Everybody just be cool. All I want is the money. The faster that happens, the quicker I'm gone. I don't want to hurt anybody," the man in the ski mask said loudly. The teller at the other window had already started pulling the money out of his drawer. Paul, who had been paralyzed until now, quickly opened his drawer and took out all that money as well. I could see his hands were shaking, and I prayed that he wouldn't do anything foolish. Just give him the money, and we'll figure out the rest later.

"Now get the money out of the other registers, and don't even think about setting off any alarms. I'm watching you." He looked at me while he was waiting. "I bet you wish you hadn't picked today to bring your husband lunch," he said, motioning at the paper bag with his gun.

"He's not my husband," I stammered. "And it's not lunch—its pennies."

He made a disgusted noise. "Who bothers with pennies anymore?"

"I do," I said indignantly. I couldn't believe this. Here I was, chatting with a bank robber, as calmly as if we were discussing the weather. "I'm collecting them for charity. Cancer research," I added.

"Do you really think you're going to cure cancer with a bag full of pennies?" he asked, his voice heavy with sarcasm.

"Maybe," I said defensively. I could feel myself starting to get angry. It must have been obvious to Paul too, as he was looking at me nervously. I could hear him now, as clearly as if we were communicating telepathically. "Please, Riley. Please don't pick a fight with the scary man holding the gun." He was probably right.

The robber rolled his eyes, shaking his head as he turned back to the tellers. "Put the money in a deposit bag."

They gathered all the bills into one bag, which Paul passed gingerly to the robber. The robber unzipped his backpack and dropped it inside. I held out my bag.

"I suppose you want these too," I said huffily.

"What are you trying to do, slow me down? Besides, those are for charity. What kind of person do you think I am?" he replied in disbelief, the gun in his hand reinforcing the irony of his statement. "You guys are doing fine so far. When I walk out the door, I want you to count to a hundred before anybody moves. Are we cool?"

We all nodded. We were definitely cool. He turned to leave but swung around and came back to the counter. For one awful moment, I was afraid he had decided to start shooting. He reached into his pocket and dropped a handful of change on the counter next to me.

"I like to do my part. For charity." I could only see his eyes and mouth through the ski mask, but I knew he was grinning.

"Thank you," I squeaked, my voice unnaturally high. He ran out the door, and I let out a breath I didn't know I was holding.

"What are you thanking him for?!" Paul exploded.

"I don't know! I was scared." My knees chose that moment to buckle, and I grabbed the counter in front of me to avoid ending up in a heap on the floor. Paul looked alarmed. He came quickly around to my side of the counter.

"Are you all right?"

Suddenly it all seemed so comical. I burst out laughing uncontrollably, which, combined with the tears running down my cheeks, must have made me look even crazier. Paul just stood there with his hand on my arm, rubbing it comfortingly. I could hear sirens in the distance, getting closer and closer. The other teller must have called the police while I was busy falling apart.

"Come over here and sit down," Paul said, guiding me toward a chair. I was still laughing and crying. I must have been a sight.

"Honestly, Riley, you're something else. You're probably the first person ever to wrangle a donation from a bank robber while he's robbing the bank! But throw in a spider, and you go to pieces." Paul was laughing now too, and I wondered if he realized he was still rubbing my arm. Not that I was complaining.

The police took about an hour questioning everyone, and it was only then that I thought about how long I'd been gone. The nurses probably thought I was smashed on the road somewhere. If I knew them, they were checking the computer to see if I'd been admitted to the ER. I located Paul, who was still giving a police officer his statement.

"I have to get back to work before the day is over. I'll see you tomorrow?" I said hopefully.

"Yeah, I'll pick you up at 7:00. Although, after today, pretty much whatever I plan is going to seem dull."

"I'm looking forward to it," I said, managing a weary smile.

. . . .

When I crept back into the office, Sarah was the only one around. She was busy charting and didn't look up.

"You're kind of starting to overstretch your lunch hour, you know. It was a madhouse in here earlier. Where have you been?"

"Believe me when I say I have a good excuse for being late." I slid into a chair, exhausted.

"You were making out with Paul, weren't you?"

"Not exactly. The bank got robbed."

"Next time I'd go with, 'My car broke down.' It's much more believable."

"I'm not kidding."

Sarah finally looked up, surveying my splotchy red eyes. "You are serious! Is everything all right? Was anybody hurt?"

"Everything is fine. As far as bank robberies go, it was pretty tame. I actually spent most of the time arguing with the bank robber."

After I told everyone the whole story, they insisted that I go home. But it was only 4:15, and I don't usually leave until 6:00. I assured them that I wasn't suffering from post-traumatic stress disorder and there was still plenty to do. So they all went about their business, leaving me at my computer. Despite my reassurances that I was fine, I couldn't seem to focus on anything.

I ended up listening to Mrs. Webster reading a story to her son in the waiting room. Her husband was in the back getting chemo, and children weren't allowed in the patient rooms; the drugs were too hazardous for them to be exposed to. It was kind of soothing in a way, like being a kid again at story time. The book was about a brother and sister who go to the carnival and play games, ride the Ferris wheel, and eat caramel apples.

I loved going to the carnival when I was young, but I couldn't recall there being one in the past few years. As I was reminiscing, it was like the last piece finally sliding into the puzzle. Why couldn't I have a carnival to raise money for the fund? It could be in October, and the whole town could come! Since September was already here, I would have to work like a crazy person to pull it all together, but think how great it would be. Maybe if things went well with Paul tomorrow, I would pass the idea by him and see what he thought.

I spent the rest of the wasted work day with my mind on cotton candy and, of course, ice cream cones. I made a note to thank Mrs. Webster for the inspiration, should the opportunity arise.

chapter 15

A man can be happy with any woman, as long as he does not love her.

—Oscar Wilde

'll have the cheese ravioli, please. No, actually I'd like the fettuccine Alfredo," I said firmly. I handed the waiter my menu, smiling apologetically. "Wait. Sorry, maybe I'd better go with the ravioli after all." The waiter looked incredibly annoyed, like it was all he could do just to humor me. I intentionally avoided looking at Paul. I'm sure he found it hilarious that I couldn't make a decision as simple as what to order for dinner.

"And for you, sir?" the waiter inquired.

"Chicken parmigiana," Paul said smoothly. The waiter nodded his approval, giving Paul a look of pity as he disappeared in the direction of the kitchen.

"I should have gotten the fettuccine," I said under my breath.

"Oh, come on!" Paul said, laughing. "I thought we were going to have to take a vote or something. It's just dinner."

"I know it's not exactly like buying a house on the scale of important decisions in life. It's just that I always get it narrowed down to two things, and no matter what I choose, I always wish I'd gotten the other one," I said, sighing and unfolding my napkin.

"So why don't you just pick the one that sounds the best, and then order the other one?" he asked, a confused look on his face.

"Because then I'd wish I had the first thing I chose." I could see his eyes glazing over. "Never mind. You can't reason your way through it, because there is no logic involved. Besides, the only reason you were so quick with your decision is because you probably order the same thing every time."

"I like chicken parmigiana—it's my default."

"But isn't that so boring, always ordering the same thing?"

"At least I know I'll like what I'm getting."

"By the way, I saw a shot of you on the news last night," I said, nibbling on a breadstick.

He groaned. "I tried to hide when I saw the cameras coming, but they were too quick for me."

"It was really no big deal; the clip was only about three seconds long." I didn't tell him that I managed to tape it and had probably rewound it forty-five times already, studying it from every angle.

"It's too bad you didn't hang around. The news crew only showed up about ten minutes after you left. They'd have loved to interview you, since you and the robber had such a pleasant conversation," he smirked.

I took several gulps out of my water glass. "No, thank you. That would have been scarier than the robbery itself. I could never be on television," I said, shuddering.

"So, no appearing on the news and no spiders. This is very revealing. What else are you afraid of, Miss Madsen?"

"You," I said. I didn't mean to say it out loud; it just sort of happened.

"Me? Why are you afraid of me?"

I cleared my throat, wishing the restaurant were darker so he couldn't see how my face flushed suddenly. "I didn't mean that I was afraid of you, exactly. I'm afraid of . . . being hurt."

I was saved from further inquiry by the waiter, who picked that fortuitous moment to arrive with our dinner. "This looks so good," I said, cutting into the ravioli and popping a piece into my mouth.

"I thought you wanted the Alfredo."

I shrugged. "By the time the food gets here, I've usually forgotten that what I ordered wasn't really what I wanted. I'm not picky—just indecisive."

"How can you say you're not picky when you don't eat meat?"

"I eat chicken. And turkey."

"That's not meat. Don't you sometimes just crave a big, juicy steak?"

I wrinkled up my nose, not bothering to answer. "How's your chicken?"

"Reliable," he said, grinning.

We were silent for a minute, both of us enjoying our dinners. "I had an idea yesterday after I went back to work, about another way to raise money for the fund."

"You're not going to start robbing banks, are you?"

I gave him a withering look. "No. I'm going to organize a carnival."

"That's a great idea! People love stuff like that. Although technically, it won't add anything to your total this year."

"Why not?"

"Well, you won't be able to get everything in order before the weather gets too cold." I think he knew from my fallen expression that he had ruined my plans. "When were you thinking of having this carnival anyway?"

"October," I said quietly.

"October? You're crazy! There's too much to do. You'd never be ready in time."

"It wouldn't be just me," I said hotly. "I know there will be plenty of people who want to help. Look at how well the ice cream fund-raiser went!"

"Riley, we're talking about finding equipment and having supplies donated and waiting for permits and rentals. It's going to be an organizational nightmare. This isn't like slapping ice cream into cones."

"I thought you'd be excited."

"I am—it's a really good idea. But your time frame is impossible. I'm sorry."

"Yeah, me too," I said, pushing away my plate.

The waiter brought the check, and I was still so disappointed that it took me a minute to notice that he was also carrying a large Styrofoam box for leftovers.

"I'm not taking mine, thank you." Since Paul had nothing left on his plate but tomato sauce, I figured it was pretty self-explanatory that he wouldn't need a takeout box either. But the waiter proceeded to set the container down in front of me. "I don't need a box, thank you," I tried again.

"I'm afraid you misunderstood. It's not for leftovers."

After Paul's rapid dismissal of my carnival idea, I was in no mood to play twenty questions with the waiter.

"Okay, so it's not for leftovers. What is it for, then?"

"Someone left it here for you, ma'am."

I glanced at Paul, who looked like he was doing his best not to laugh.

"Is this a joke? Am I going to open this lid to find a big hairy spider inside, programmed to jump on me?" I demanded.

"I have no idea what this is about. I'm just a spectator."

I carefully opened the lid, cringing as I peeked inside.

This was not happening. Not on my date with Paul. Inside the takeout container, I could barely glimpse a hint of pink paper, drowning in a sea of pennies. I quickly closed it again, before he could see what was inside.

"Who left this for me? What did they look like?"

"I really couldn't say," the waiter replied nonchalantly.

"Why couldn't you say? Did he make you promise not to? Did he pay you off?"

"No, ma'am. I couldn't say because he was gone before I arrived. I didn't see the gentleman."

"But it was a man?" I prodded.

"Yes, ma'am," he said, departing as soon as he could.

Paul sat across the table, smiling broadly.

"What are you grinning about? Is this funny to you?"

"I still don't know what it is. But the way you reacted—yes, I find that amusing."

I glanced around nervously, but everyone seemed to be

innocently eating their dinner.

"What are you looking for?" he whispered.

"Someone is following me."

"What—like a stalker? There's not a dead rabbit in that box, is there?"

"No, not a stalker. Just . . . someone."

"Something less sinister, then. Perhaps an admirer?"

My head snapped up, instantly suspicious. "Why did you use that word? What do you know about all this?"

"Its simple deduction: if he's not stalking you, that limits the other options significantly. He's probably just obsessed with you."

"That's silly. Of course he's not in love with me," I said, brushing it off.

Paul cocked his head. "I never said he was in love with you—I said he was obsessed. That's an interesting leap you just made."

"I didn't mean he was in love with me. It was just a slip of the tongue," I said, flustered.

"Well I think he's very bold, leaving you a present when you're on a date with another guy."

"It hardly qualifies as a present."

"What's in the box, anyway?"

"It's full of pennies."

Paul laughed out loud. "This guy definitely knows the way to your heart," he said, his voice taking on a sarcastic tone.

"What's that supposed to mean?" I asked, the volume rising with every word.

"Well, come on—pennies? It's not very romantic, is it? I like to think if I were leaving someone a secret gift it would be something more impressive than spare change."

"I think it's sweet. Should we go now?"

"Don't you want to hang around, scope out the restaurant? He could be anyone. He could be our waiter!"

"I think you've gotten just about all the mileage you're going to get from this," I said tartly.

"Okay, I was just trying to be helpful."

I picked up my box full of pennies and followed Paul to his car in silence. He opened my door and I got in and fastened my seat belt. He drove back to my apartment, neither of us saying anything. When he parked the car, he fiddled with his keys, sighing.

"Why do you get such a kick out of making fun of me? I thought we were past that," I said finally.

"I didn't mean to make fun of you. It was just so . . . embarrassing."

"Embarrassing? You weren't the one being presented with a box full of pennies by the waiter!"

"Yes, exactly. It doesn't say much for me that you're being pursued by some mystery guy while we're on a date. How can I compete with that?"

"Paul, I was on the date with you, not him. You don't have to compete with anyone." I reached out and put my hand on his. Where this brave impulse came from, I'm not sure. But he smiled, entangling his fingers with mine. He leaned toward me, our eyes fixed as he brushed the hair away from my face with his free hand. He lightly touched my lips with his, an ethereal ghost kiss that was composed more of imagination than anything else. He started to move away, but I pulled him back, kissing him this time.

When I opened my eyes, he looked dazed. "Thanks for dinner," I said, suddenly feeling very shy.

"I'm sorry about earlier. In the future, I'll try to be less jealous. Good night."

"Good night, Paul." He drove the car down to a further building, where I guessed he lived. I'd never been in his apartment. The word *jealous* hung in the air like a fine mist. Paul was jealous of the Penny Guy. Never in my wildest dreams did I imagine I would have not one, but two eligible guys, both interested in me at once.

I walked into my apartment and set my box full of pennies on the kitchen table. I took a deep breath before lifting the lid and unearthing the pink slip of paper. I unfolded it, reading the words slowly.

> You are kindhearted and luminous, full of light.
> He doesn't deserve you.

The memory of kissing Paul, still fresh in my mind, clashed with this lovely compliment from a stranger. What was I going to do?

. . . .

When I arrived at work on Monday, the schedule looked pretty light. This is never a guarantee of how the day will really go, but it's a good start. After I got the charts pulled for the next day, I started making a few preliminary calls. I wasn't ready to throw in the towel on the idea of the carnival in October just yet. I called Krista, the woman in HR who helped me organize the ice cream fund-raiser, to see if she had any connections. My biggest problem was going to be location. I knew that people would be happy to donate time and supplies, but if we had no place to hold the carnival, nothing else really mattered. I also called Paula to see if she'd mind hitting up the ice cream supplier again. She promised she would do her best, and she seemed thrilled about the idea of a carnival. That was about as far as I went before we got busy.

In between patients, my doubts began to surface. Maybe I was just kidding myself, thinking that I could pull this together in a month. I started thinking about all the planning involved, and it wasn't long before I was feeling pretty down about the whole thing. People took months to plan stuff like this. Plus, there was all the red tape. I had casually mentioned the idea of a carnival to my mother on Sunday, and she commented that it takes forever to process the permits. I never imagined there would be so much paperwork to wade through. I guess I was thinking more on the level of a lemonade stand, not a huge charity event.

The longer I thought about it, the deeper I sunk into my chair, and the more I thought Paul was right. I'm surprised Krista didn't laugh out loud when I suggested it. She was probably just being kind. I was glad that I didn't tell more people, so it wouldn't be quite as embarrassing if the whole thing came crashing down around me.

The door chime sounded, announcing yet another person who required my assistance. But it wasn't a patient. It was the UPS guy.

He was red-faced, struggling to lift a medium-sized box from his wheeled cart. He glanced at my name tag briefly.

"I'm guessing you're the Riley I'm looking for," he grunted, trying to balance the box without falling over. "I don't know what this is, but I hope it's worth it. I think I threw my back out lifting it off the truck."

I reached across the counter to take it from his hands, the sheer idea of that much weight not really registering in my brain until my arms gave out. I dropped the box unceremoniously onto the counter in front of me.

"Boy, you weren't kidding," I said, just grateful that both my arms were still in their sockets where they belonged. "Why is this addressed to me? I don't do any ordering."

He shrugged his shoulders. "Good luck getting that to your car," he called out as he left with his cart.

By now, there was a fair amount of nurses standing around. Anyone who wasn't already here before had appeared, alerted to the fact that something was up due to the impossibly loud thud when I dropped the box.

"What could it be? You don't think it's anything dangerous, do you?" Andrea asked, shrinking away involuntarily. With all the excitement, I hadn't seen my boss come in to join everyone else.

I put my ear to the box for a minute, straining for any sounds. "Well, it's not ticking. I'm gonna open it."

The box was addressed to Riley Madsen, c/o Landmark Hospital Cancer Treatment Center, but there was no return address. I used the scissors to break through all the packing tape, finally managing to pry open the lid. Inside was a black garbage bag, secured tightly with a twist tie.

"I hope it's not a human head," I said lightly, untwisting the tie. I peered inside the bag where, to my amazement, rested thousands of pennies. Sarah leaned over my shoulder, trying to see into the bag.

"Is that . . . a box of pennies?" she asked incredulously.

I was speechless. I sunk both hands into the warm copper pool, burying them deep, coming up with palms full of coins. I plunged them in again, feeling something foreign in the depths.

I pulled out a folded piece of pink paper and noticed how quiet it had suddenly become in the room. Like everyone realized what an important moment this was. We all stood together, collectively holding our breath. I opened the note and read it through slowly once, then again.

"Well? What does it say?" Sarah asked impatiently, her voice booming in the surrounding silence.

Clearing my throat, I read, "One who admires you greatly is hidden before your eyes."

Everyone just stood there, mulling it over.

"Wow," Kate said finally. "This is getting huge. Everyone knows about your project now, Riley, and they all want to help."

"Yeah," Sarah smirked. "Apparently, some more than others. I'd say this guy has a major crush on you," she said, folding her arms in front of her chest and leaning back in her chair smugly.

I rolled my eyes. "Come on, he's just trying to be nice."

"Right. That's why he enclosed the poetry on *pink* paper with his contribution. I bet you it's only a matter of time before you hear from him again."

"Well . . . " I said hesitantly.

Sarah leaned forward suddenly, planting both feet on the ground and smacking me on the arm. "This isn't the first time, is it? Why didn't you tell us? How do you know it's the same person?"

"The pink paper," I admitted sheepishly.

"I knew it! Riley has a secret admirer," Sarah said in a singsong voice. Everyone started chiming in with their opinions on who the mystery guy could be, but the speculations were cut short by the sudden rush of patients. Everyone went about their business, leaving me to stare at my computer. I found myself mesmerized by the screensaver, my eyes stuck while my mind raced. A voice behind me startled me from my zombie-like state.

"Think about it, Riley—he probably paid more for the postage than the pennies are even worth," Celeste said in a rare moment of clarity. "He must really like you." She paused to let this sink in before leaving to pick up something from the pharmacy. I resumed my position from before, zoning out and wondering just who was scrawling the pink notes that were stealing my heart.

chapter 16

We all suffer from the preoccupation that there exists . . .
in the loved one, perfection.

—Sidney Poitier

So, I had this idea about another way to raise pennies. I thought
it was a really good plan, but everyone I know seems to be
working overtime to convince me that it will never work."

Lauren and I were folding sheets in the laundromat on a
Friday night. Every time someone opened the door, a chilly breeze
drifted in, the first sign that fall was setting in. Before you know it,
the first snowflakes are sticking to the ground and winter is here.
This thought depressed me, and I wasn't sure why. Fall is a beautiful time of year, and I love Christmas. Still, I felt down.

Whether it was the carnival disappointment or the impending cold weather, I felt like going back to my apartment and not
coming out again until April. I often think I should have been
born a bear. When it starts getting cold, bears eat and eat until
they nearly explode. Then they crawl in a cave and sleep it off for
several months. Yes, the bears know how it's done.

"Well, tell me your plan," Lauren said, interrupting my hiber-
nation fantasy. "You know there's nothing I like better than one of
your half-baked schemes."

"I thought we could host a carnival. We'd charge admission,
in pennies, of course. And we could get local businesses to donate

127

food and prizes—we'd make a fortune. Remember the carnival the city used to hold in the fall? I wonder why they stopped doing that," I mused.

"Well, I don't see what's not to like about your idea. I think it's fantastic! Where's the problem?"

"We'd have to do it before it gets cold, and everyone says I'd never be able to pull it together in time. Paul said I was crazy."

"Well, you are—that's one of the things we all love about you," Lauren said, shaking out a towel before folding it perfectly. "Where is Paul tonight, anyway? Shouldn't you be out painting the town with him instead of doing laundry with me?"

"We're going out tomorrow. I told him I had something really exciting planned for us."

"Oooh, what are you going to do?"

"I have no idea. I was totally bluffing. Any great suggestions?"

"You could drive to Vegas and get married."

"Not quite that exciting, thank you."

"You can't tell me you haven't thought about it."

"What? Marrying Paul? Lauren, we've been out twice."

"Yeah, but you've known each other for a while now. It's not like you just met."

"That doesn't exactly make me feel better. Most of the time I've known him we've spent arguing. We seem to fight at the drop of a hat."

"So you fight sometimes. That just means you get to make up later," she said with a mischievous grin.

"I'm not sure we've really progressed to that point of the relationship."

"But you guys did kiss, didn't you?"

"Sort of."

"Sort of? How exactly do you 'sort of' kiss someone?"

"I don't know. It's complicated," I hedged.

"Riley, I remember when you met this guy. He absolutely infuriated you, yet I could tell that at the same time, you were completely attracted to him. The only reason you wouldn't be turning cartwheels now that you're finally dating him is if there were someone else." Her voice trailed off, and I watched a stunned look of realization steal across her face. "There's somebody else, isn't there? Who is he? Why haven't you mentioned him?" she asked eagerly.

"Remember I told you about the pennies on my car seat, the day of the ice cream fund-raiser?" I filled her in on the recent developments.

"This is so romantic and sweet! What does he look like? Is he cute?"

"The thing is, I've never actually met him. I think that's why they call them 'secret' admirers."

"Riley," she said disapprovingly. "I know you're not thinking of brushing off Paul in exchange for a total stranger. You don't know anything about him."

"I know he's very kind, and he cares about other people. And he has beautiful green eyes."

"You've just described my grandfather perfectly. But that doesn't mean he's the right guy for you. Paul is real. He's here, and he wants a relationship with you."

"Paul is . . . flawed."

"They're all flawed. The point is, you have to find one whose flaws you can cope with. This Penny Guy isn't perfect either. I promise."

"Relax, Lauren. I like Paul a lot, and I'm not ready to make any decisions right now. It's just exciting to have this mystery guy, making all these romantic gestures," I said wistfully.

"I don't like this, Riley. I don't like this at all," Lauren said, shaking her head.

"Oh, you're just jealous because I have two wonderful guys and you only have one."

"One is more than enough for me. Speaking of which, how does November 30th strike you?"

"For what?"

"My wedding, silly."

"November 30th, as in this year? As in, less than three months away?"

"That's the one."

"And Paul thought I was crazy! You'll never have time to pull it all together."

"We just want a simple wedding, so there won't be that much to plan. And I don't want to wait any longer than that."

"But what's the rush? What makes you so much more certain now than the first time he asked you, or the second, or the seventh?" I pressed.

She paused, searching for the right words. "I think I finally realized that the reason I kept turning Stewart down was because I was afraid."

"Afraid of marriage?"

"Afraid of being happy. Sometimes it's easier to stick with what you're used to, even if it's disappointment. But I decided that I was ready to take a chance on happiness with Stewart, and I'm ready to get started."

"You know, sometimes you are very wise."

"I'm going to need a lot of help from my maid of honor," she warned.

"You can count me in."

. . . .

"Where are we going?" Paul asked, fidgeting in the seat next to me.

"I told you, it's a surprise. Can't you just chill out?"

"It's hard to chill out when you have a blindfold on. I've never even seen your driving before. My life could be in constant peril, and I wouldn't even know it." He kept scratching around the blindfold. You'd think from the way he was acting that I was an entire gang of thugs who'd violently kidnapped him, depositing him roughly in the trunk of the car before speeding off into the night.

"Paul, you're making me nervous. Are you really that uncomfortable?"

"It's this blindfold; it's making me all itchy."

"It's silk."

"Well, maybe I'm allergic."

"Yeah, you probably have the lesser known but very serious silk allergy I was just reading about."

"Maybe it's paranoia then. I can't help being afraid that I might accidentally fall asleep like this and wake up in Canada."

I'd been driving around aimlessly for about fifteen minutes, trying to make him disoriented. Obviously it was working, perhaps a little too well. I got the distinct feeling that Paul was coming to the end of his patience with me, and we all know that never ends well. "All right, Moody Pants, you're almost free," I said good-naturedly as I parked the car. "You just sit there for a minute, and don't you dare peek."

I got out of the car, walked around to the trunk, and pulled out the picnic basket. I went to the passenger side and opened Paul's door, amused to see that he was still fiddling with his blindfold.

"Oh, just take it off already. Honestly, I can't believe you're fussing this much." He didn't need to be told twice, tearing it off and rubbing his eyes furiously. He finally opened them cautiously, peering around while they adjusted to the light.

"Where are we, anyway?" he said, stepping out of the car and stretching his long legs.

"It's only the park. Why do you keep looking around like we just landed on the moon?"

"I can see it's the park, but why are we here?"

"Flag football," I said sarcastically, holding up the picnic basket.

"I hope that's food, because I'm starving."

"There's a good spot over there," I said, pointing to a grassy spot under a tree. I spread out a blanket and started unloading the feast. There were sandwiches and potato chips and sodas, and I baked an actual apple pie for dessert. I left it in the trunk as a surprise, for later. Unfortunately, I didn't realize that there wasn't any mayonnaise for the sandwiches until I was making them. Paul did okay for a while, but toward the end, I could tell he was having a hard time choking it down. There's not enough soda in the world to wash down turkey on wheat with no mayo. It's like trying to swallow sandpaper.

"Sorry about the sandwiches. I didn't realize I was out of mayo until it was too late."

"No mayo? Really? I hadn't noticed," he said, taking another giant gulp of his drink.

"You finish your sandwich. I'm going to go get the dessert." I ran off in the direction of the car, happy to have something to dull the unpleasant memory of the sandwiches. I grabbed the beautiful pie out of the trunk and started back with my prize.

"Ta da!" I said proudly, setting the pie in front of him with great ceremony.

"Wow. That looks delicious," Paul said, amazed.

"What I lack in sandwiches, I make up for in pies."

"What kind of pie is it?"

"Apple," I said, slicing into the nicely browned crust.

"I love apple pie. Cut me a great big slice."

I slid the perfect slice of pie onto Paul's plate and handed him a plastic fork. He took a huge forkful off the end and chewed thoughtfully while I anxiously waited. His initial look of anticipation quickly changed to one of surprise, then polite disgust.

"What? Is it not good?" I said, taking a bite of my own slice and quickly spitting it discreetly into my napkin. Paul actually swallowed his, by some superhuman feat of strength.

"I must have mixed the salt up with the sugar," I said finally.

"I'd say that was a fair assumption, yes. But, if it helps at all, it looks incredible. It's too bad there isn't someone you really hate that you could give it to."

I tried not to think about how everything was falling in around me. I pulled a loaf of bread out of the picnic basket and started twisting off the tie.

"I'm sorry, Riley, but I couldn't eat another bite."

"It's not for you. It's for the ducks," I said, trying not to sound as cranky as I felt.

"I don't know how to break it to you, but I don't see any ducks," he said, looking around in all directions.

"There's a duck pond down there."

"Where?"

"Down that hill over there."

"If there were ducks down there, wouldn't we hear them . . . quacking?"

"I used to come here all the time when I was a little girl, and I remember that at the bottom of that hill is a duck pond. Are you coming with me or not?" He took the loaf of bread that I thrust at him, and we walked down the hill without speaking.

This really wasn't going as well as I'd hoped. I pictured Paul being really excited about my surprise destination, but the only thing he'd shown any real interest in was the picnic basket. The sandwiches were dry, the pie was a failure, and now we were wandering around, looking for a duck pond that I could tell Paul didn't believe existed.

To my dismay, the only thing at the bottom of the hill was a small playground.

"Maybe it was another park," Paul said helpfully.

"It used to be right there," I said, pointing at the unfriendly little swing set and slide. I walked over to one of the swings and flopped down. "Why do things have to change? First Lauren, then the duck pond. This whole evening has been a catastrophe."

Paul came over and eased into the swing next to mine, chuckling.

"In case you were unsure," I told him, "this is not a time for laughing. I find no humor in this . . . disaster."

"Riley, aside from the salty pie and the vanishing duck pond, I don't see what you're so worked up about."

I looked at him in disbelief. "Everything went wrong! In fact, you should be grateful I didn't have any mayo for the sandwiches. With the way my luck has been going, we both would have ended up with food poisoning!"

"Well, I think this is a really good date. We're on the swings, which is like recess, and that was always the best part of any school day. Except lunch, that is. My mother always used to make me these roast beef sandwiches with about an inch of mayo on them—that was her secret ingredient . . . "

Before he could finish, I leaned in and kissed him hard on the lips. He wove his hand through my hair until I finally pulled away, breathless.

"What was that for?" he questioned, a look of surprise etched in his features.

"For trying to make me feel better."

"But not succeeding?" he said wryly.

"You did very well," I said reassuringly.

"But . . . "

I sighed tragically. "Lauren's getting married."

"I'm afraid you've lost me. Isn't that a good thing?"

"It's great. I'm really happy for her."

"You're a terrible liar."

"Most of me is very happy for her. But there's a little selfish part of me that can't help feeling a little . . . "

"Jealous?" he said simply.

As hard as I tried, I couldn't stop the tears that immediately sprang to my eyes. I didn't trust my shaky voice, so I only nodded. Paul reached across my swing, the comforting weight of his arm around my shoulder. The gesture had the effect of lowering the last reserves I was clinging to.

"All I can think of is how it seems like she has everything I ever wanted, and she never even tried! What kind of a friend am I? I'm going to have to put on a smile and go to her wedding all alone. And the worst thing is, I'm going to lose my best friend," I sobbed.

"You don't have to be by yourself, you know," Paul said finally.

I brushed the tears away the best I could. Now that the flood of emotion was subsiding somewhat, I realized how pathetic I must have sounded. "What do you mean?" I quavered.

"I'll go with you . . . to Lauren's wedding. If you need a shoulder to cry on, I'll be there."

"Really?"

"I promise," he said firmly.

"I'll probably get your suit all wet."

"I think I'll manage."

I took a ragged breath. "Thank you for listening to my little breakdown. I don't know why I'm telling you all of this. I wouldn't blame you if you ran as fast as you could in the other direction."

The sky was a shocking deep midnight blue, lightening to a pale yellow at the edges where the sun most recently departed. I was glad I'd worn a sweater; it suddenly seemed quite chilly. I shivered.

"Are you cold?" Paul asked.

"Just a little bit."

"Maybe it's time to go, before it gets too dark to find our way back to the car." He tentatively took my hand as we stood from the swings, a pleasant tingle rising from my fingertips.

"Look, it's the first star!" I said, pointing into the vast sky. "Did you wish on stars when you were little?"

"I think that's more of a girl thing."

"I always made the same wish, but it never came true."

"That's incredibly depressing."

"Oh, I don't know. There's still time." I paused, closing my eyes to make my wish.

"What did you wish for?"

"I can't tell you, or it won't come true."

"If past experience is any indicator, it won't come true anyway."

"Well, I'm not taking any chances."

. . . .

After I dropped Paul off, I went home and got into the shower. I was just drying my hair with a towel when the doorbell rang. It was 11:30—something had to be wrong. I ran to the door, not bothering to check who it was before flinging it open. Strangely, there was no one there, which was just as well, since I was in my bathrobe.

The sole occupant of my front step was a plastic grocery bag, tied with a pink ribbon. I looked around curiously, knowing that he might possibly be out there somewhere, watching. He probably was long gone already. I bent down and picked up the bag, closing the door and locking it behind me.

I opened the bag, not at all surprised to discover that it was full of pennies. The ever-present pink note rested on the top, and I unfolded it eagerly.

> I heard you were searching
> 'Round town for a place,
> To host your occasion—
> Not any old space.
> But one that will hold
> All who come through the doors.
> The location is mine—
> For one night, it is yours.
> Expect a call very soon.

I stood in amazement, my mouth gaping open. I dashed to my phone, and sure enough, there was a message. My heart was beating so loudly, I wasn't sure I would be able to understand the words.

"Hi Riley, this is Krista. Sorry I missed you. I've been putting off calling you back because I didn't have any good news for you. I planned on calling you today anyway, just to bring you up to speed. But right before I picked up the phone, a man called me from Administration to inform me that someone volunteered a property for you to use! The only condition is that the owner wishes to remain anonymous. It's absolutely perfect, Riley! You must have a guardian angel or something. Call me tomorrow, and I'll go over the details with you, okay? I can't believe we're really going to do this! Bye!"

I listened to the message again and then reread the note. I did this about three times before it finally sunk in. I went to bed, but all I could do was lay there, making a mental list of who I needed to call the next day. The last thing I remember thinking before finally drifting off to sleep was that I wanted to call Paul first, to give him the good news.

chapter 17

The grand essentials of happiness are: something to do,
something to love, and something to hope for.

—Allan K. Chalmers

It was official. The carnival was a go. Krista would take care of all
the paperwork. She was used to setting up events for the hospital,
so she knew how to do things properly. I was so relieved when
she just took charge of that end, since the red tape was the part that
really scared me. I was going to focus on getting donations from local
businesses—food, prizes for the games, that sort of thing. Krista
would arrange most of the equipment as well. The hospital owned
several white tents, like the one we used for the ice cream fund-raiser.
They also had plenty of tables and chairs, and Krista promised that
anything they didn't have, she would take care of. It was a good
thing I had her and her resources on my side. Otherwise, I probably
wouldn't have gotten any further than the planning stage.

Any spare moments I was left with were devoted to helping
Lauren plan her wedding; sleep was but a distant memory. Going
with her to choose a cake and pick out a dress brought back painful memories for me, but I pushed them away and forced myself to
make this about Lauren, not me. I wanted her to have only happy
associations with her wedding.

Almost every minute that I wasn't occupied at work was spent
organizing donations. Where I once frittered away my downtime

shopping online, I now made calls to businesses. I was floored by the willingness of everyone I came in contact with. Most of the people I approached gave at least something, and many gave more than I would have dared ask. And everyone seemed to have a story. Either they'd lost a loved one to cancer or were in the process of watching someone fight it. Some had survived their own battle. It seemed that every life was touched by this terrible disease in one way or another.

Paul was a big help getting ready for the carnival. He completed every task I gave him, and even a few I didn't. One day he stopped by the office unexpectedly to see me. He was so excited because he'd talked a local bakery into pledging thirty dozen doughnuts. His eyes gleamed with pride, like a little boy who cleaned his room without being asked. All the nurses congratulated him, spoiling him with offers of soda and cookies from the stock we kept for the patients. He was the man of the hour, and I was happy to say that, for the moment, he belonged to me. Everyone told me how lucky I was after he left. "Isn't he sweet?" and "He's so gorgeous!" I had to admit they were right.

Paul and I were getting closer, but we still did a fair amount of snapping at each other as well. Sometimes he said such thoughtless things that it was hard to remember why I put up with him, but I'm sure I had my moments as well. Still, we always managed to come around to being friends again, and as usual, Lauren was right about the making up part. We had definite sparks, but I couldn't help feeling he was holding something back.

We hadn't really discussed our past relationships, as if those were parts of our lives that were off limits. If the conversation ever drifted in that direction, we both went behind our individual fences, conveniently posted with KEEP OUT signs. Every now and then, I found myself wanting to protect him, to be the one who made sure that no one could hurt him again. Maybe that's what love is, but it was still too early to think about that.

The carnival would be held on October 27, and there was a little less than a month left. With so much still remaining to do, I worried constantly that we'd never be ready in time. But just when I was ready to throw up my hands and declare the whole thing hopeless, someone would step in with an amazing donation or volunteer to help with something I couldn't find time for. I fell into bed every night exhausted, but I'd never been more excited about something in my life.

With the latest proceeds from the office pig, plus the change from the jars in the grocery store, the total was $961.19. If the carnival went even half as well as I expected, we were going to finish the year off with a bang.

. . . .

"Oh, Riley, I'm glad you're here. I've got something for you." My grandmother walked over to an antique armoire, wrenching open one of the massive drawers. She pulled out a crocheted afghan with an intricate design, feathered with blues and greens and browns. "I made this for you to raffle at your carnival."

"Grandma, this is beautiful. I don't know where you found the time." She waved her hand, dismissing it as if it were nothing.

"Once you get the hang of it, they go really fast. No trouble at all. By the way, I've got that bag of pennies I was telling you about too." She loaded the large Ziploc bag into my other arm.

"I should have brought you something—I feel a little guilty," I said, trying to juggle both armloads.

"It's just spare change from the ladies in my quilting circle. When I mentioned what you were doing, they were happy to have a chance to help." She wandered off into the kitchen to stir something on the stovetop. It's funny, but I can't remember ever being in my grandmother's house when there wasn't something simmering.

"Guess what I found the other night?" I called into the kitchen.

"What?" she said, tasting something from the pot with a spoon.

I pulled the penny out from where it was hidden under my shirt. She squinted from across the room, trying to decide what my treasure was. She walked over to me and took the penny in her wrinkled hand. She rubbed the surface, perhaps trying to turn back the clock to happier days. For a minute, she was somewhere else entirely, her eyes dreamy and faraway.

"I found it hidden in a box, in my closet. I'd almost forgotten about it. It's strange how something so meaningful can be put aside and lost for years."

"Yes, it's easy to lose sight of what's important."

"I remember that day like it was yesterday. I was so afraid that you would come out and catch us. I just knew you were going to have a fit when you discovered the giant hole in your driveway."

Her laugh animated her whole face. "Oh, I knew all about it. He was more excited about it than you were, I think."

"It was all so unbelievable—like something you might read in a story. I was flabbergasted when I broke the dirt apart and found that penny," I said, shaking my head.

"Your grandfather loved you so much, Riley. Your finding that penny didn't happen by chance."

"What do you mean?"

She sighed as if she were suddenly bone tired, her breath catching in her throat. "You were his first grandchild, and he wanted the two of you to have something special to do together. One of the men whose car he fixed gave him a handful of old coins, and he buried that penny when you were still a tiny baby. Even then, he was planning how one day you would discover it together."

There were tears on my cheeks, but I didn't realize I was crying until my grandma handed me a tissue.

"Sometimes I can't believe it's been that many years that he's been gone. He would be so proud of what you're trying to do, just like I am."

"Thank you, Gram. That means a lot." I hugged her, experiencing an urgent, fleeting feeling of transience. It was one of those moments where your mind takes a snapshot, because you know that you will never be in that place again. Someday, you will want to take it out and study it, smoothing the edges bent with time.

....

When I got home that night, I checked my messages. I had missed a call from Paul.

"Hey, Riley, it's me," he said comfortably. I couldn't believe we were already to the "it's me" stage of the relationship. "You're probably still out, collecting donations for the carnival. You must be tired; you've been working too hard lately. So, I'm going to wait while you go get into bed." Pause.

Was he serious?

"I'm serious! Go get into bed!" Amused, I carried the phone into my bedroom and crawled into bed, fully clothed. "Are you there yet?"

"Yes," I said to no one.

"Good. Now, snuggle down into the covers." I did as I was instructed, pulling the blankets up to my chin. I couldn't believe how sleepy I was. I'd be lucky to stay awake long enough to hear the end of the message. My eyes drifted closed as I waited for him to continue.

"Okay, here's your bedtime story."

I smiled. "Once upon a time, there was a princess named Riley, who was very sweet and kind. She spent all her time trying to think of ways to help people who were sick. In fact, she spent so much energy trying to save the world that everyone began to fear that she might become ill herself. So, her handsome boyfriend decided to do something special for her birthday."

At the word *birthday*, my eyes popped open. "Well, that's all really. Keep that evening free, okay? Good night, princess."

My birthday. I had hoped everyone would forget.

chapter 18

There is still no cure for the common birthday.

—John Glenn

A re you sitting down?" Lauren asked breathlessly.

"You're standing right next to me. You can see I'm sitting down."

"Sorry, my brain is working on an entirely different level right now. I just had an epiphany, something that can only be described as sheer brilliance," she said, sliding into the chair across from me.

"Well? What is this brilliant revelation?"

"Frankly, I'm not sure you're prepared for it."

"Oh, spill it, already!"

She paused for dramatic effect. "Paul . . . is the Penny Guy." She held out her hands, waiting for me to congratulate her on her genius.

"I'm sorry to spoil your grand moment, but Paul is not the Penny Guy."

"Why not? It makes perfect sense. You started getting the pennies right around the time you and Paul started dating. I don't know why it took me so long to figure it out. This is so romantic; I can't believe a man actually came up with it. It just goes to show you, they can be sweet when they want to be, but most of the time, they just can't be bothered."

"Lauren, there's one gaping hole in your theory. Paula, the lady at the snack bar, told me that the Penny Guy has beautiful

142

green eyes, whereas Paul has lovely blue ones."

"Maybe he wore colored contacts. Or he could have used a decoy to throw you off the trail."

"How do you explain the fact that he was so jealous when that waiter brought me those pennies at dinner?"

"He's acting! He wants you to think that it's someone else."

"I think you're getting a little carried away. If this were a fairy tale, Paul would reveal himself as the Penny Guy, and we'd live happily ever after. But this is real life."

"Why can't you just admit that it might be Paul?"

"Don't you think I've considered the possibility? Don't you think I want it to be him? I've fantasized over and over again about Paul coming to me in different scenarios. 'Yeah, you know that guy that's been leaving you incredibly romantic poetry and pennies everywhere you go? Well, you don't have to be confused anymore, because it's me! I'm the penny guy! Let's get married and ride off into the sunset!' " I paused to catch my breath. "Things like that don't really happen," I said quietly.

"Riley, I know you're convinced that there are no happy endings. But just what if it was Paul?"

I sighed, the doubts planted by Lauren beginning to creep into my brain. "Wouldn't that be something?" I said in a tiny voice.

"Yes! That's all I needed to hear!" she said, hugging me and squealing like a little girl.

"I didn't say it was him. I just said it was possible," I grumbled. A thought suddenly came into my head, and my eyes narrowed. "Do you know something I don't? Are you on the inside?" I demanded.

"I'm only speculating. You know me—I couldn't keep a secret to save my life. I just imagined the most perfect possibility I could come up with and ran with it."

"Yeah, I guess you'd crack under the pressure. You wouldn't beat around the bush if you really knew anything; you'd rent a billboard and tell the world."

"So true. While we're on the topic of cracking under pressure, I have something to tell you that I feel really bad about."

She looked away, but not before I caught a glimpse of the guilty expression on her face.

"Come on, whatever it is, it can't be that bad."

"But it is! Stewart is taking me to Nebraska to meet his parents."

"I know that people say in-laws are horrible, but they can't be that bad."

"No, it's not that. He's already bought the plane tickets, and it's the same weekend as the carnival. Do you hate me?" she pleaded.

"Of course I don't hate you."

"Maybe we could exchange the tickets for another date . . ."

"Lauren, it's not like you're brushing me off to go to the movies or something. You're meeting your future in-laws; it's really important. I understand."

"Are you sure?"

"Positive," I said reassuringly.

"Would it help if I bought you a strawberry shake?"

"Well, it's a start."

"Good. Let's go get a huge strawberry shake and talk some more about how your boyfriend is living a double life."

. . . .

"I'll have the orange chicken, please. No, actually I'd like the chicken lo mein. Oh, maybe I'd better stick with the orange chicken after all," I said, unable to look at the waiter as I hung my head in shame.

"Sweet and sour pork," Paul pronounced easily.

I sighed, a little louder than I intended.

"Let me guess," Paul said. "You really wanted the noodles."

I nodded. "It's unfortunate that I am incapable of making simple decisions where food is concerned."

Paul pushed his chair away from the table. "I'll be right back. I'm just going to find the restroom."

While Paul was gone, I reached into my purse, taking out my compact. I touched up my lipstick and wondered for the umpteenth time if Lauren was right. Maybe Paul was the Penny Guy. Maybe he was going to tell me tonight.

Paul sat down across from me, snatching one of the egg rolls in the middle of the table. "You didn't have to wait for me," he said as he demolished it in three bites.

"I didn't even notice the waiter had brought them," I admitted.

"What were you thinking about when I sat down? You were completely zoned out."

"Nothing—my mind was just wandering." The waiter appeared with a tray of food. He set the sweet and sour pork in front of Paul and placed the orange chicken and the chicken lo mein on my side of the table. My eyes bulged. "I'm sorry, there must be some mistake," I started.

"No, everything is just fine, thank you," Paul said firmly.

I stared at Paul with a blank look.

"What?" he said, his mouth full of food.

"You told the waiter to bring both things?"

He tried not to smile. "Trust me, it's easier this way. Happy birthday!" He forked a piece of my orange chicken.

"Not so loud!" I hissed. "The next thing you know, they'll all be over here . . . singing!" I glanced around anxiously, keeping an eye out for lurking waiters.

"Relax! I kept your secret, just like you asked. What is it with you and birthdays, anyway?"

"I don't like getting older," I said simply.

"Riley, you're twenty-four. I'd hardly call that old."

"That's not the point. There are all these landmark ages when you're growing up. But really, what is there to look forward to after twenty-one?"

"I've never really thought about it like that before. You've cheered me up immensely. Well, I guess I'd better start working out more, taking my vitamins."

"Why?"

"You might decide to replace me with a younger man. I'm twenty-seven. That's practically on the downhill slide."

I smirked at him, noticing for the first time the solitary fortune cookie the waiter brought with the food. "Um, why is there only one cookie?"

"Maybe you'd better open it."

"How will we know which one of us the fortune applies to?" I said, cracking it open.

"I'm pretty sure it's for you."

I unfolded the tiny paper.

> It shouldn't be hard since your head's full of brains,
> Go to the place where they keep all the trains.
> (For more INFORMATION, see Hugh at the station.)

"I'm guessing this isn't your average fortune cookie," I said, looking completely cool on the outside while my brain went into overdrive. It was a clue, in poem form. He was so the Penny Guy! "So, we're going to the train station."

"Really?" Paul said cryptically, his face devoid of any telltale expression.

. . . .

As we entered the train station, I was struck by how enormous it was. People everywhere, all scurrying like ants to get to their destination in time. To my right was a desk with a large sign that declared INFORMATION in bold red letters.

"I think that must be the place." As we neared the desk, I could see the man at the counter had a name tag, stating that he was, in fact, Hugh.

"Can I help you?" he asked with a kind smile. He was a rather fragile gentleman who looked to be about 105.

"My name is Riley," I said uncertainly. "I think you might have something for me." He reached into a drawer, coming up with a small key labeled 79B, and pressed it into my palm.

"Anything else?" he asked politely.

"You tell me," I said jokingly.

He laughed like that was the funniest thing he'd ever heard, and we disappeared into the banks of long brown lockers. It took me a minute to locate 79B, but the key slid into the lock perfectly. The only thing inside was a slip of paper.

> I'm not a great poet, so you're out of luck.
> Go to the place where there are no more duck(s).

I looked at Paul in amazement. "I can't believe you did all this." He blushed, looking very pleased with himself. He took my hand as we walked out of the train station.

"How do you feel about a stroll around the park?" he asked casually.

. . . .

My mind was going a million miles a minute in the car on the way to the park. Paul just kept smiling, like the cat that got the canary. Like a man with a secret. Lauren must've been right.

How did she always know? If Paul really was the Penny Guy, this opened up a whole new realm of possibilities. I flashed back to all the little surprises he'd left me and how he pretended to be so hurt and jealous at the restaurant, when the pennies were from him all the time. I would have to act surprised when he revealed his secret identity. I didn't want to disappoint him after all the trouble he'd gone to.

"Here we are," he said, parking the car. "Now, what?"

"Well, there's this charming little duck pond I'd like to show you. It's at the bottom of that hill."

"Lead the way."

Swimming in the gravel on the playground were several yellow rubber ducks. I gathered them up, discovering one with a message tied around his neck.

"Well, what do you know? There are ducks down here!" Paul exclaimed, as I unrolled the message.

> Here they sell spiders; don't get in a rage.
> You're safe, 'cause his eight legs are trapped in a cage!

"Spiders in a cage. Ugh. That must be a pet store," I said, shuddering. "But there are lots of pet stores. How do I know which one?"

"The duck knows. Go on, ask him."

On the underneath side of one of the ducks, I found a sticker with an address on it.

. . . .

The pet store was busy for a week night, mostly full of children begging for fish or hamsters. There were some glass tanks along one wall, inhabited by lizards, frogs, turtles, and . . . tarantulas. As we got closer, I could see a piece of paper rolled up and tied with a ribbon, resting against the edge of the tank. A large, hairy tarantula prowled the perimeter, and my stomach dropped as I realized that the paper was on the inside of the cage.

"Oh, come on. You've got to be kidding me," I said, pointing to the next clue, just out of reach behind the glass.

"Well, I suppose the question is, how bad do you want it?"

"Paul, there could be a hundred-dollar bill wadded up in there and I still wouldn't go anywhere near it."

"Maybe I should have a go," he said, ever so slightly lifting the edge of the lid.

"You put your hand in there with that thing, and you can forget about touching me ever again!" I said firmly.

A man came over from behind the register. "You must be Riley. Perhaps I can be of assistance." He had a large leather glove on one hand, which he used to retrieve the note from inside the tank.

"Thank you," I croaked, taking the paper between two fingers like it was diseased. I unrolled it gingerly, hoping to avoid any spider germs.

> You've walked the path with danger fraught
> And emerged, braver than you thought.
> Go to the place where you were born
> And look for the spot where the ground is torn.

"The place I was born? The hospital?"

"Hey, I'm just the driver!" Paul said, opening the car door for me.

. . . .

By now, it was dark outside. When we got to the hospital, Paul took a flashlight and a shovel out of the trunk.

"Paul, you can't just go around digging up public places! Are you trying to get us arrested?!"

"I've already gotten permission. Do you think I'm crazy?" He handed me the flashlight, which I immediately switched on. "This is kind of creepy. I feel like a grave robber or something," he said, slinging the shovel over his shoulder.

I stopped, shining the light right into his eyes. He stumbled back a step, wincing. "Why don't you lead the way? The sooner we dig up the clue and get out of here, the happier I'll be," I said sweetly.

"Look over there," he said, pointing. In the far corner of the courtyard, there was a suspicious-looking patch of fresh dirt. He handed me the shovel, which I held, dumbly. "What are you waiting for? Start digging!"

"Me?" I squeaked.

"It's your treasure."

It only took a minute to shovel the dirt aside, the earth still soft from being recently moved. I uncovered a box in the hole and lifted it out and brushed off the dirt.

This is it. It's all happening too fast. The box is going to be full of pennies, and Paul is going to confess. I took a deep breath, carefully easing off the lid to find . . . a silver chain. I didn't even have to act surprised. I took it from the box, holding it up in the moonlight to see a tiny silver star dangling on the end. I didn't know what to say.

"It's like the star you always wish on," Paul explained. "You wished on it that night at the park, remember? I remember, because it was the first time I knew I was falling for you." He jammed his hands into his pockets, staring at the ground.

"Paul, it's lovely. Thank you. This whole night—I can't believe you set this up just for me." He took the necklace from my hand and fastened it around my neck. I watched as he filled the hole with dirt, and I tried to shake off the feelings of disappointment. It's not that it wasn't a thoughtful gift—it just wasn't what I was hoping for. It's like when you open the last present under the Christmas tree, and it's a sweater. It's a nice sweater, but what you really wanted was a CD player.

· · · · · · · · · · ·

I sat on my bed that night absently fingering the star on the chain. I was really lucky. Paul was a great guy. So why did I feel let down? I told myself that Paul could still be the Penny Guy. Maybe he just wasn't ready to tell me yet. I pulled down the covers and got into bed, switching out the lamp on my night table.

I was just drifting off when the doorbell rang. I flew out of bed, running to the door and flinging it open. But there was no one there—just an enormous bouquet of probably fifty pink balloons bobbing around on my front step. The balloons were tethered by a Ziploc bag full of pennies, the pink note nowhere to be seen. I dragged them through the front door, which turned out to be a lengthy process, since they all really wanted to explore the world outside instead of being confined to my apartment.

I sifted through the pennies, but there was no note. I began popping balloons, hoping that none of my neighbors would call the police to report that shots were being fired. As luck would have it, I only had to kill four balloons before I found the elusive pink note.

"Looking back, I have this to regret, that too often
when I loved,
I did not say so."
—David Grayson

Happy Birthday, Riley

I pinned the note on the fridge with a magnet, as I had done with the others. The notes, along with the remaining balloons, made my kitchen look cheery. But I still felt inexplicably sad. I turned out the lights and went back to bed.

chapter 19

Love does not begin and end the way we seem to think it does. Love is a battle, love is a war; love is a growing up.

—James Baldwin

With only a week to go before the carnival, I had a terrifying call from Krista telling me that one of the local news stations wanted to do an interview with me. I told her that she was the PR lady and she should handle it. But she said that they wanted to talk to me, since I was the one who started the whole penny thing. They thought it would be a great little human interest story. Even as I was repeatedly telling Krista no, I knew I was going to have to do it. I couldn't pass up that much free publicity, and what better way to get people interested than a spot on the evening news?

I grudgingly said yes, after much persuading on Krista's part. She told me I had nothing to worry about; it would be a two-and-a-half-minute blurb at the end of the news, pre-recorded in case I forgot how to speak or had a sudden heart attack.

. . . .

"Riley, you're going to do great! Just think about it; you can do anything for two and a half minutes. Piece of cake," Sarah said nonchalantly.

"Do you have any idea how long two and a half minutes really is? Try holding your breath and you'll see what I mean."

"You have to do this, Riley. Think how many people will see it."

"You're not helping."

"You know what I mean. This is a great opportunity."

"If it's so great, then you do it."

"Yeah, that would be impressive. 'Hi, my name is Sarah. I'm one of the nurses who work with Riley Madsen. She couldn't be with you today, as she is currently hyperventilating under the table.'"

"See, you're a natural! I really appreciate this."

"You have to do it, Riley. You started this, and now you have to finish it."

"I know," I said in my smallest voice.

"Good. Now, when is it?"

"Tomorrow," I said glumly, lowering my head into my hands.

"Terrific! That's far enough away from the carnival so that people won't have plans yet, but close enough that they won't forget," Sarah said brightly.

"You've really thought of everything. Are you sure you don't want to do it?" I asked hopefully.

. . . .

I hid in the bathroom in the lobby of the news station, trying to ignore my shaking legs. This was ridiculous. Why didn't I just say no when they asked me? The thought of being on television filled me with a dread I couldn't describe . . . maybe even worse than spiders. I took a deep breath and walked out of the bathroom and directly to the front desk. There was an impeccably groomed woman waiting for me.

"Riley Madsen?" she said, sticking out her hand.

"Yes?" I peeped, my voice high and unnatural.

"I'm Hillary Richards. It's so nice to meet you," she said, shaking my limp hand firmly.

"Thank you for having me. What am I supposed to do, exactly?"

"Well, first off, relax. This really isn't as bad as you think. You sit across from me and answer my questions. Try to keep your responses brief and to the point because you don't have a lot of time." I must have looked like a mouse trapped in a corner, with the cat closing in. "Trust me; it will be over before you know it." She patted me on the arm, and we walked down a short hall that led to a room with two chairs and several hundred insanely bright lights.

No matter how I tried, I couldn't make my legs move to follow her through the door. My feet felt about a hundred pounds each and cemented to the floor. By now, Hillary had discovered that I was no longer behind her. She turned around and came to get me. She grabbed my arm firmly at the elbow and guided me toward the chair, where I flopped down, my unsteady legs no longer willing to support my weight. Hillary smoothed her skirt and eased into her chair, crossing her legs and smiling.

"Are you ready?" she asked cheerfully.

This was never going to work.

"I think it's best to plunge right in. No need to sit here and stew, right? All you have to do is be yourself. And smile—this is a good thing you're doing, and you look like you're in a prison interrogation room!"

I could feel the nausea rising, but I pushed it down and managed a weak grin. The man behind the camera was making some adjustments, and the other people milling around scurried to their corners. Five, four, three, two, one . . .

"For our last story tonight, I have something guaranteed to make your heart melt. With me is Riley Madsen. Riley, tell us a little about your story." She leaned back in her chair with a serious look, waiting.

My story? What does she mean by that? Where does she want me to start? Why didn't I rehearse this at home? My mouth was so dry, I wasn't sure the words would come out, even if I could form them. *Say something, Riley. You only have two and a half minutes!*

I forced myself to smile. "Well, it all started on New Year's Eve. I was tired of making resolutions that I never kept. So I decided that this year, I would set aside all my pennies until the end of the year."

"And what happens then?"

"Well, I work in a hospital where we treat cancer patients. I decided that I would donate my savings to cancer research."

"That is very generous of you," she said sweetly.

I felt my face turn hot and red. "Well, it's not just me. Since I started, people from my family, work, even total strangers have started approaching me with their pennies. Everyone wants to help—it's incredible. The people in our community are so generous and giving. Without them, it would just be me and a big jar of pennies," I said sincerely.

"So, you're here to tell us about an event?" Hillary prodded, trying to keep me on track.

"Yes, we've had numerous businesses and individuals agree to donate their time, talents, and supplies for a carnival, which is going to be held on October 27th at 2:00. Admission is two hundred pennies, or two dollars, a person. There will be all kinds of fun things to do and treats and games, and we hope to see you all there."

"That sounds great. If someone couldn't make it to the carnival but was still interested in helping, what could they do?"

"You can donate to the Riley Madsen Cancer Research Fund, which is set up at the Cedar Hills Bank."

"Well, Riley, it was so nice to meet you and hear your story, and we wish you luck with your pennies. If you are interested in more information on the carnival, you can go to our website. That's all we have time for tonight. We'll see you tomorrow." Hillary kept her cheesy grin plastered in place until the camera guy made a signal, which I guess meant we were finished.

It was over. I survived.

"Riley, you did so well! No one would ever know I had to drag you out here!"

"Once I got going, the words just came out," I said in amazement.

"You should be very proud. Before you go, I have something for you." She reached behind her chair to pull out a large canvas tote bag full of pennies. "Everyone at the station chipped in. I was going to give it to you during the show, but things were going so well that I completely forgot. I hope it helps."

"This is wonderful. I can't believe how many people have stepped up with donations."

"Well, I have to be going, but maybe I'll see you at the carnival."

"You're coming?" I said, unable to keep the surprise out of my voice.

"Of course—my kids will love it. Good luck, Riley."

. . . .

My cell phone rang the minute the news was over. It was my mother, calling to congratulate me and tell me how thin I looked on TV. That's the great thing about my mom—she always knows just what to say. When I hung up with her, the phone rang again.

"Well, well, Miss Madsen. For someone who said she could never be on television, you did remarkably well. I was a little worried at the beginning, but you found your tongue eventually," Paul said, smiling. Even over the phone, I could tell he was smiling.

"It's over, anyway. That's all I care about."

"So, what time do you want me there Saturday morning to help set up?"

"Actually, we're going to get most of the tents up Friday night. Are you in?"

"Just let me know when and where. I'm willing to help with anything . . . except the clowns."

"What's with the clowns?" I asked curiously.

"I think clowns are creepy, that's all."

"It's a costume. It's not like they're aliens or something."

"How would you like to be confronted by a guy in a giant spider costume? Wouldn't that terrify you?"

I giggled. "Actually, that would be pretty funny."

"Well, I'll take on any task you want, as long as you keep your clown on a leash."

"I'll make sure no clowns cross your path."

"Clowns plural? There's going to be more than one?"

"Yes, they generally work in gangs, and I'm told they can sense fear. So, look them right in the eye and make sure they know you're the boss. And under no circumstances should you *ever* run from a clown, because he may attack."

I could feel him glaring at me on the other end of the line.

. . . .

On Friday night, I had my first glimpse of the spot where the carnival would be held—a wide stretch of farmland that wasn't currently growing much of anything. I was struck by how remote it was, for being so near the city. The land was bordered on one side by a line of trees, their leaves painting the sky in fall colors. Toward the back of the property was a faded red barn with a hardwood floor. There was going to be an old-fashioned country dance in the barn at night after the carnival ended. We would even have live music; Sarah had arranged for her cousin's bluegrass band to perform.

Paul was already there when I arrived, helping set up tents and booths. I tried to pitch in, but it was one of those occasions where you fear you are hindering the process more than helping. We were only there about an hour because so many people showed up, and we left early to go home and get some sleep so we would be fresh for the next day.

When we got back to the apartment, I yelled to Paul, who was getting out of his truck at the opposite end after dropping me off.

"See you in the morning!"

"Yup. Try to go to sleep instead of pacing the floor and stressing out, okay?"

Yeah, right. I gave him the thumbs up and went inside.

. . . .

I really did try to sleep for a while. But I could only stand staying in bed until about 6:30. I put on a sweater and jumped into the car, certain that I would be the first one there. But when I arrived, people were already busily going about their tasks.

It was like watching an enormous jigsaw puzzle being pieced together, one item at a time. I hadn't seen Paul yet; he was probably still asleep.

I walked around to various areas, trying to be of some use. For a while, I helped sort pumpkins into different piles, according to size. A local farmer donated part of his crop, to be carefully examined and purchased by children of all ages. The pumpkins ranged in size from the smallest gourd to some mammoth specimen that would have required several men to lift them.

There was also going to be a booth for face painting, a pie eating contest, and a farmers' market, stocked with donated produce. I also worked on a maze for the younger children, constructed with hay bales. It was tall enough that the kids wouldn't be able to see over the edges, but short enough that the adults could watch. I was happy to see my favorite carnival game from when I was a kid—the fishing pond. I loved dangling my hook over the edge, because you never knew what you would get. There was also a wishing well, built by Paul's friend Jack so you could throw in your penny and make a wish.

And then there was the food. There was popcorn and stands lined with plastic bags filled with pink and blue puffs of cotton candy. There were rows of caramel apples, some dipped in nuts, standing tall and proud on sheets of wax paper. There were huge grills for roasting endless cobs of corn, which would be dipped into vats of hot melted butter. I could almost smell the warm deep-fried scones, dripping with gooey honey butter. There would also be apple cider and hot chocolate to warm everyone up when it started to get cold. And, of course, ice cream.

I admired a long table displaying all the handmade donated items for the raffle. Tickets were fifty pennies each, with the drawing at the end. I helped out where I could, doing odd jobs and trying to manage any last-minute emergencies.

I saw the van from the bakery drive up to deliver the doughnuts, which reminded me that there was still no sign of Paul. Where could he be? I made a quick call to his cell phone but was met only with his answering machine.

"Hey, sleepyhead, it's 11:00! What happened to you? Call me when you get this, okay? Bye." Before I had a chance to start worrying, the truck from the ice cream distributor arrived, and I helped unload the tubs into the waiting coolers.

. . . .

At 3:00, the party was already in full swing. There were quite a few people so far, and they all seemed to be having a good time. Children darted through the crowd with painted faces, and I was excited to see Kimberly from the bank helping out at the face painting booth. She told me that Paul recruited her. I asked her if she'd seen him, and she said no. We chatted while she fashioned me a cat face, complete with whiskers and a pink nose.

I saw my family for a minute, making their way through the crowd. They couldn't stay very long, because Mitch had a football game later. Mitch complained that he would rather just stay here and eat cotton candy instead. My parents both hugged me, telling me what a huge success it was. I kept searching the throng of people, hoping to see Paul. I really wanted him to meet my family. But there was still no sign of him.

Clowns wandered with clumps of balloons in every shade imaginable, dispersing them to the children. Everywhere you looked, there was a balloon bobbing in the sky, the string clutched in a tiny hand. It was funny to watch the children's different responses to the clowns. Some smiled, pointing at the funny red noses or enormous shoes. Others were terrified, crying and screaming until their bemused parents took them away.

I felt a hand on my shoulder, whirling around to see Paul.

"Where have you been?" I sighed in relief. "Did something happen? I was worried."

"I'm really sorry. Something came up."

"That's it? Something came up? I was thinking you must be lying in a coma somewhere."

"I didn't plan to be so late—it just happened."

"Whatever. I don't have time to do this right now," I said coldly. Now that I knew he was okay, I couldn't believe how livid I was.

"Riley, I really am sorry. Put me to work. What can I do?"

He really did look repentant, but as far as I was concerned, it was too little, too late. I couldn't believe he'd blown off something that was so important to me, with only a vague explanation and minimal remorse.

"Go ask around. I'm sure there are plenty of things you can help with."

He kissed me quick on the cheek and headed out into the crowd, eagerly searching for redemption.

The rest of the day was made up of a million different moments that all blurred into the night. There was an overload of images to see and consider, and I filed them away for later, when I would have time to reflect on them individually. I saw Paul on and off during the day. He brought me a spider balloon animal that had a message tied around its neck. "Are you still mad at me?"

I reluctantly gave him a half smile. "I could never be mad at you, Mr. Spider."

"Not the spider! Me! How are you feeling about me?" Paul asked.

"Oh, you are far from off the hook."

"Riley, I had to approach an actual clown to get this balloon animal. Doesn't that mean anything? Tell me he's not frightening," he said, pointing to a clown on the edge of the crowd.

"Oh, I don't know, he doesn't look too bad. Do you want me to step on him for you?" I asked.

. . . .

The families were disappearing into the gravel parking area, carrying sleeping children, stuffed animals, and various other carnival spoils. The dance was beginning, and people were making their way to the barn, which was covered in strings of lights. The music drifted from the door into the brisk night, where I was helping to dismantle one of the tents.

"Did you save a space on your dance card for me, pussycat?" Paul's voice drifted nearer.

I'd forgotten my face was painted. "I'm working. There's a lot left to clean up," I said coolly.

"Come on, one dance. I promise there will still be plenty of work to do after that."

I allowed Paul to lead me toward the barn, fighting the impulse to just forgive him and have a good time. I wasn't through being mad yet. A slow song started, and we joined the other couples, spinning around the floor. A sad fiddle took turns with a harmonica, weaving their way into the lonesome rafters. I leaned on his shoulder, feeling him relax.

"So, what really happened today?" I asked quietly.

He sighed. "Can't we just have this dance, and talk about it later?"

"That's just it—you act like it's no big deal. Well, today was a big deal for me. You said you would be here, and you weren't. I could understand if you had a good reason, but you act like you can't even be bothered to explain it to me. So, tell me. What was so important that you couldn't even call to tell me you were going to be late?"

"I had to drive an old friend to the airport."

"Really? And you just found out about it this morning?"

"Yes, she called me and needed a ride."

"She? This wouldn't happen to be an old girlfriend, would it?"

He avoided my gaze, which probably could have burned through an acre of forest. "Yes, she was my girlfriend, before you. Remember the flowers on Valentine's Day? She had a couple of hours before her flight, and she wanted to talk."

I pushed away from Paul, shaking my head in disgust. "I don't believe this. You deserted me today so that you could walk down memory lane . . . with an old girlfriend?"

"We didn't end very well before; there was no closure. I wanted to say good-bye. Surely you can understand that," he said, clearly frustrated.

I was furious. "What I can understand is that you had your choice of where you wanted to be today, and who you wanted to be with. And you chose." I stormed out of the barn, bulldozing my way through the mass of happy couples.

"Riley, wait," I heard Paul call out behind me. I turned around and shot him a look that told him he'd better steer clear of me for a while, and he gave up, walking in the other direction toward the parked cars.

. . . .

I walked around in a daze among the remains from the festivities. The dance was clearing out, and everything was almost put back in order. The ground was nearly bare, the only lingering signs of our inhabitation being the recently trampled dirt. I felt as empty as the land around me, like all the feelings inside me had been torn down along with the tents and booths. I alternated between wanting to cry and feeling seething anger and disappointment. What about Paul's old girlfriend? Was today really good-bye, or would he just pick up where he left off . . . with her?

I heard hesitant footsteps behind me. I hoped that it wasn't Paul, even as I found myself praying that it was. I probably wasn't ready to see him just yet. It was a fine line between breaking down and forgiving him and breaking off little pieces of him.

"Hello, Riley. I'd appreciate it if you didn't turn around," a voice whispered.

I froze. The night had turned chilly, and he was standing near enough to me that it was easy to imagine I could feel the heat radiating from his body.

"How are you enjoying the carnival? Is this not the most beautiful spot you could ask for?"

"Who are you?" I asked, moving to turn around.

"I really wish you wouldn't do that," he said softly. "I kept my end of the bargain, and you must do the same. The one condition for you to use my property was that my identity remains secret, remember?"

"You're the one that snuck up on me. I didn't seek you out."

"I couldn't help it. You looked so sad, and on a night when you should be celebrating. I was hoping there was something I could do to help."

"Well, that might be a little bit difficult. As you just stated, according to the rules, you have the right to remain invisible. Perhaps if you told me who you are . . ." I trailed off.

"But you know who I am, Riley. I'm your secret admirer."

"Maybe you could be a little more specific."

"I'm surprised you don't recognize me, not to mention a little hurt."

I blinked, my eyes widening. "Should I?"

He leaned a little closer. "I know you very well," he said, his breath on my neck combining with the cool night air to cover my arms in goose bumps.

"Well, I'm afraid you have me at a disadvantage then, because I don't know you at all."

"Oh, you know me. You just don't realize it yet."

"Why don't you enlighten me?"

"The time isn't right. But you will know soon." His hand brushed my arm briefly, and I glanced down at it, trying to fix this solitary clue in my mind. "Good night, Riley," he said, the sound of my name on his lips vaguely familiar. And then he was gone. I spun around to see a man in a clown costume, disappearing into the darkness.

Although at times I thought I'd heard his voice before, it was never above a whisper, so it was impossible to really be sure. But there was something I did know. I had only one other piece of evidence to work with: his hand, and there were two things that unnerved me about it. First, that I was certain I'd seen it before, although I couldn't match it to anyone specific. And second, I was nearly positive that it didn't belong to Paul.

chapter 20

Jealousy, that dragon which slays love under the
pretense of keeping it alive.

—Havelock Ellis

It was frigid in my bedroom when I awoke the next morning. I shivered as I tugged at the quilt folded at the end of my bed, pulling it up to burrow underneath. As I snuggled deeper into my covers, I caught a glimpse of movement through my window. I was shocked to see snowflakes drifting down, making a white blanket against the fallen leaves. A surprise snowstorm at the end of October—a day earlier, and the carnival would have been ruined.

The carnival. That one word brought back a whole parcel of memories, both delightful and disturbing. After the fight we had, I couldn't believe that there wasn't a message from Paul on my answering machine when I got home. Maybe he decided I wasn't worth all the trouble. Or maybe talking things over with his ex-girlfriend yesterday made him realize he still had feelings for her. Either way, neither scenario had a very appealing end for me. I had the feeling I was soon to be back at square one, and I had come to a very important decision.

No more blind dates. No exceptions. I was tired of being set up with an endless string of guys with whom being single was the only thing I had in common. No more, "That was fun—we should do it again sometime," with both of you knowing that you can't ditch each other fast enough. I was through with blind dates; I didn't need any extra frustration in my life. And no more dating bank tellers either, as a matter of principle.

While we're on the topic of frustration, there was the Penny Guy. I still couldn't decide whether he was someone worth pursuing. He was definitely sweet. I had an entire refrigerator covered in pink notes to prove it. And being so near him last night, I felt certain there was an attraction between us. It's too bad I couldn't fuse Paul and the Penny Guy into one perfect man, who was both physically and emotionally available.

I lay in bed for a long time, watching the snow and enjoying the peaceful, quiet morning. I finally decided that if I didn't get up, I was going to be late for church. So, I threw the covers off in one swift movement, feeling the cold air hit me like an icy wall. I ran for the hot shower.

. . . .

When I got home from church, I hurried to check my messages and was ecstatic to find one. But it wasn't Paul; it was my mother. She called to tell me that they would be eating dinner at 5:00, if I wanted to come. She'd put a roast in the Crock Pot and had thrown in a nice piece of chicken for me, if I was interested.

Why not? Why should I sit around moping all night, waiting for Paul to call? I changed my clothes and drove home, where I had a nice piece of chicken, mashed potatoes, homemade rolls, green beans, warm brownies studded with walnuts, and several games of Go Fish before I sped back to my apartment to check my messages. There was only one, from Lauren. She said that she was having a great time and she was sorry she'd missed me, since she was dying to hear how the carnival went. She promised to try me again, as soon as she got a minute.

Still no call from Paul.

I sat on the couch with a bag of cheese puffs, watching TV until I felt drowsy. I finally gave up and took my orange cheese-covered self to bed.

. . . .

Sarah was waiting to pounce on me Monday morning before I even had a chance to take off my coat.

"So? How much?"

"How much what?" I asked, unwinding the scarf from my neck.

She rolled her eyes. "Honestly, it's like having a conversation with the family dog. How much money did you make at the carnival?"

"I don't know," I said truthfully. "Krista said she would call me when they knew the total."

"But it was a lot, right?"

"Yeah, I think we did pretty good." I sighed, sinking into my chair.

"What's wrong? You should be on top of the world, but you look like you lost your best friend."

"It's nothing," I said, brushing her off and pretending to be really interested in my blank computer screen.

"Riley . . . "

"Paul and I had a big fight, and I met the Penny Guy. Well, I sort of met him. I talked to him, but he was wearing a clown costume with a mask, so I still don't know who he is. And Paul hasn't called me, so I'm afraid he may be thinking about hooking up with his ex-girlfriend," I blurted out. Sarah was the first person I'd had the chance to unload on, since Lauren was out of town and I really didn't want to have this discussion over family dinner on Sunday.

"Slow down, Riley. Let's just focus on one tragedy at a time. What makes you think Paul is going back to his ex?"

"He was really late getting to the carnival, but he wouldn't tell me why. I finally managed to weasel out of him that the reason it took him so long to get there was because his ex-girlfriend needed a ride to the airport. She conveniently had a couple of hours before her flight and she wanted to 'talk,' " I said angrily.

"So he blew you off to have a heart-to-heart with his ex?"

"Exactly! Thank you! Why is it so hard for him to understand how wrong that was?"

"I don't know—it's like guys are operating from an entirely different manual."

"And then, when I stormed out, he didn't even try to stop me. Well, he didn't try very hard, anyway," I said grudgingly.

"And you said you met the Penny Guy?"

"I was out walking around after my confrontation with Paul, and I heard someone coming up behind me. But he had on a costume, so I couldn't tell who he was."

"Maybe it was Paul," Sarah said hopefully.

"I don't think so. There was something familiar about him, but I'm pretty sure it wasn't Paul."

"So, did you talk? What do you think of him?"

I hesitated. "I'm not sure. There's definitely something . . . intriguing about him."

Sarah smiled suddenly. "You like him, don't you?" When I didn't say anything, she grinned even more. "You do! I can see it all over your face. Well, there is something exhilarating about having a secret admirer, but what about Paul?"

"Paul and I were doing so well. I really felt like we had a connection. But I guess it's kind of up to him."

"And if Paul comes back and apologizes? If you have to choose?"

I sighed heavily and shrugged my shoulders. I didn't have an answer for that question.

. . . .

I got home from work that night determined to avoid calling to check the messages. I made myself a turkey sandwich with plenty of mayonnaise and ate half of it before I gave in and picked up the phone.

No messages.

I polished off the sandwich and started rummaging through the freezer, looking for ice cream. I located the carton of butter pecan, not bothering with a bowl but deciding instead on the direct approach. My spoon and I were making some significant progress when the doorbell rang. I considered just pretending I wasn't home, resigned to suffer death alone from ice cream overdose. But my curiosity took over, and I reluctantly plodded to the door.

On my front step, there was Paul, holding two large cups with steam pouring out of the slots for sipping.

"Hey, can you believe this weather? It's a good thing it didn't come a few days earlier," he said, holding one of the cups out as a peace offering. When I made no immediate move to take it, he said, "It's hot chocolate . . . with whipped cream." I finally reached out and warily took it from his hand.

He smiled that hundred-watt smile of his, assuming that he was almost back into my good graces. But it wasn't going to be that easy. He took a sip of his drink and shivered. "Look, I know I'm in the doghouse, but do you think we could discuss it inside?" I stepped aside and held my arm out in a gesture that would have been welcoming, if not for the sarcastic overtones.

Paul stomped the snow from his shoes and stepped inside. He looked around my small apartment, surveying the furnishings. I wondered what he thought he could tell about me from how I decorated. "So, this is it," he said.

"Yup. This is it."

"It's nice. There's something kind of familiar about it. I feel like I've been here before."

"Could it be because the floor plan of your apartment is virtually identical?"

He snapped his fingers. "That must be it."

We stood in my living room/kitchen, the awkwardness in the air as palpable as if we were meeting for the first time.

"You're not drinking your hot chocolate," he commented.

"That's because if it's as good as it sounds, I'm afraid I'll forgive you."

"That was the general idea."

I tentatively took a sip, the rich chocolate warming me all the way down to my stomach.

"Well?"

"It's really good, but I'm not sure it's making me like you any better. Do you want to sit down, give it a chance to kick in?"

He sat on the loveseat, patting the cushion next to him. I perched myself on the chair across from him instead.

"So, how much money did the carnival raise?" Paul asked, changing the subject.

"I don't know the total yet. Krista said she would let me know as soon as it was all counted."

"It looked like there was a good turnout."

"Yeah, everybody really pitched in and worked hard," I said, unable to keep the bitterness out of my voice. I quickly swallowed some more of the hot chocolate, hoping some of the sweetness would rub off.

"Riley, I told you I was sorry. I don't know what else I can say."

"Let's see. How about, I'm sorry I didn't bother to call and let you know where I was so you didn't have to worry all day? I'm sorry I chose to spend the day hanging out with my ex-girlfriend instead of being there when you needed me. I'm sorry that I'm probably going to break your heart, just like every other guy you've ever met."

Paul looked bewildered, and he opened his mouth to speak, but no words came out.

"I thought you were different," I said, staring at the cup in my hand.

"Okay, I admit that I should have called. It's just, suddenly I had a chance I never thought I'd get—a chance to close a door on something in my past, and I took it. When Trisha broke up with me, all I got was a message on my answering machine, telling me that she needed space to figure some things out, and not to try to find her. After dating her for two years, that was all the closure I got. That was on Valentine's Day. I planned to ask her to marry me that night."

As angry as I was with Paul, I felt my insides turning into marshmallow.

"I hadn't heard from her until the morning of the carnival. She said she needed a ride to the airport, and she wanted to talk. She wanted to apologize for the way she left things, sort of clean the slate before she married someone else."

"She's getting married?" I asked hollowly.

"That's why she was going to the airport. She was flying to Hawaii for her wedding. But I shouldn't have let you down on a day that was so important to you. It was a mistake. And as for the bit about breaking your heart, maybe you're right about that too."

"What?"

"Well, I can't promise that I'm never going to do stupid or careless things, because I will. I'm only human, and there are going to be things that we won't agree on. I'm going to do things that will disappoint you, but that doesn't mean I don't love you."

I was all ready to burst in with my rebuttal the moment there was a pause in the conversation, but Paul's last words stopped me dead in my tracks.

"Wait a minute. Say that last part again," I whispered.

He looked confused. "The part about how I'm going to disappoint you?"

"No, the other part."

His eyes were the bluest blue I'd ever seen them. He leaned forward, meeting my gaze directly. "I care about you, Riley. A lot. I think I'm falling in love with you."

"Really?" I said, my voice cracking.

He nodded his head. I stood up and walked over to the couch, sitting down next to him. "You're not just saying that because you knew I'd go all melty and forgive you, right?"

Paul laughed. "I wouldn't dare." He drained the last of the hot chocolate from his cup and looked around for a garbage can.

"There's one in the kitchen," I said, handing him my cup as well. He took them both and disappeared around the narrow wall that separated my tiny kitchen from the living room. I felt a tremendous wave of relief wash over me. Maybe everything was going to be okay now. With the ex out of the picture, we could just pretend it never happened.

"Riley?" I heard Paul's voice, muffled by the wall.

"Can't you find it?" I called back, amused.

"No, I found it. I found these too," he said, appearing with several pink slips of paper. He held them up so I couldn't possibly miss them, and I felt my stomach drop. "Care to explain?" he said sweetly.

. . . .

"Paul," I started.

"No wait, let me guess. These are from your secret admirer, right?"

"No big earth-shattering revelation there. You knew about him already."

"I knew he left something at the restaurant for you . . . once. But it looks like there was a lot more to it than that."

"It didn't mean anything," I said lamely.

"Well, if it didn't mean anything, why did you save all the love notes he left you?"

"Paul, they're not love notes. You're overreacting."

"I'm overreacting? I can't believe you gave me such a guilt trip over spending a few innocent hours with Trisha when you were carrying on this whole secret relationship behind my back!"

"It's not a relationship. I don't even know who he is!" I shot back.

"Do you think that makes it better?" He ran his hand through his hair roughly as he paced around the small room. "No wonder we're not getting very far—it appears your feelings are already committed elsewhere."

"I can't believe you're going to make me the reason we're having problems."

"Well, if the shoe fits . . . "

"I should have told you, but there was really nothing to tell. I can't help it if this random person is obsessed with me. I certainly didn't do anything to encourage it."

"I agree that it's not your fault that this guy has a thing for you. But you didn't have to build a shrine to him in your kitchen either."

I couldn't think of anything to say to that, and although I knew this flirtation wasn't nearly as serious as Paul thought it was, there was still some truth in what he was saying.

"If you can honestly tell me that your only response to the gifts and poems from this stranger was feeling flattered, and that you never weighed him against me and wondered if he might not be just a little better, I'll drop it and never bring it up again," Paul said finally.

I felt terrible, but I couldn't lie to him. I couldn't even look at him. He walked to the couch and sat down next to me. He lifted my arm, turning my hand over and using his hand to smooth my palm out flat. He put the notes into my hand, closing my fingers around them.

"When you figure out what you want, let me know, okay?"

Before I could say anything, he was gone. I heard the door close behind him, having the sensation that as he left, he took all the air in the room with him. I was sealed into a tiny space where I couldn't breathe. I'd never thought of my apartment as too small before, but suddenly the walls seemed built directly around me. I knew I had to get outside where I could breathe again.

I jumped off the couch, shoving my feet into shoes and making a dash for the door. The chill outside was colder than I expected, but I didn't really feel it. I didn't bother with a jacket. I just wanted to get as far from my apartment and that room with no air as I could.

. . . .

I'm not sure how long I wandered around, but eventually the shock must have worn off. My teeth were chattering, and lack of air seemed an appealing option when compared with freezing to death. I started back in the direction of my apartment as quickly as I could. I had to end this thing with the Penny Guy, but I wasn't sure how. Paul was the one I should be with—he was real, and he said he loved me. I should have told Paul that part of the reason I allowed myself to feel something for this stranger was because, deep down, I thought it was him. That thought made me feel better, and I resolved to rid myself of any evidence of the Penny Guy as soon as I got home.

I rounded the corner that led into the parking lot, eager to get inside and take a nice long shower. It was hard to tell at that distance, but I thought I could see someone at the door of my apartment. My heart started beating faster. Maybe it was Paul! I quickened my step, my shoes crunching in the snowy slush that had frozen when the temperature dropped. The person at my door looked around suddenly, like an animal being tracked in the woods, like he was afraid of being caught.

I ducked behind the hedge, trying not to move. My breath came out in icy puffs, betraying my presence in the cold night air. I peeked over the top of the bush I was hiding behind and saw the man take one more look around before returning to his task, which appeared to be hanging a holiday wreath on my front door. It had to be the Penny Guy.

This couldn't be more perfect. I will catch this guy, and then I'll see he's only a man, and I can move on. I can tell Paul honestly that I don't have any feelings for the Penny Guy.

I crept a little closer, ducking behind the next hedge, then making my way slowly toward my door. I was almost behind him now, and I could see the wreath was made of pennies, a pink note dangling from the center like a smoking gun.

As I eased onto the first step leading to my door, the salt on the pavement crunched, the noise deafening in the wintry silence. I saw the Penny Guy's entire frame tense, frozen in place. He must have known he was caught, but he didn't turn around. After what seemed like an eternity, he said, "Hello, Riley. I guess the game's up." He swiveled around slowly, and I gasped as I confronted the awful truth in those beautiful green eyes.

"Hello, Brian," I croaked.

I sat at the kitchen table, surrounded by stacks of wedding invitations, pristine white envelopes, stamps, and address lists. One of my sisters teased me, saying that I should hire someone to address the envelopes so that everyone wouldn't look at the handwriting and suspect they were written by a kindergartner. I crossed the names off the address list as I went, unconsciously filling the room with my happy humming. The wedding was only a few weeks away now, and although it had seemed at the beginning that the preparations would never be complete, everything was finally falling into place.

I resisted the temptation to creep into the closet to look at my wedding dress. I loved to run my fingers along the delicate satin, fingering the intricate beaded pattern on the train. My one regret was that I only got to wear the dress for a single day; certainly the festivities should be spread out over at least a week.

I continued carefully addressing the envelopes, wanting everything to be just perfect. The doorbell rang, and I hurried to open it.

"Finally! Where have you been, slacker? You're going to have to help with something where this wedding is concerned, you know." I kissed my handsome fiancé before taking his hand and dragging him into the kitchen, where I forced him into a chair and pushed a stack of envelopes toward him.

"Now, you're not leaving until you've addressed some of these envelopes. And no sloppy writing—they have to be perfect. Can you be trusted, or would you rather lick stamps?" I said teasingly.

"Riley, there's something I need to tell you."

"Well, talk while you're stamping. Be a multi-tasker."

His hand reached over, moving away the stack of envelopes I was working on. "It's important," he said urgently, focusing on the envelopes so he could avoid the look of growing alarm on my face.

"What's wrong? What is it? Is everybody okay? Was there an accident?"

"Everybody's fine. It's nothing like that," he said soothingly, covering my nervous hands with his strong ones.

"You're scaring me, Brian. What's wrong?"

"I don't know how to tell you this, but I don't think we should get married."

I let out a huge sigh of relief. "That's just cold feet, honey. Everybody gets cold feet; it's not serious. You just have to hang in there—it'll be fine, you'll see. When the wedding is over, you'll wonder why you were even worried." I went back to addressing envelopes.

"It is serious, and it's not cold feet. Riley, there's somebody else."

My hand, which was so meticulously laboring to form the perfect lettering, stilled, and I raised my eyes to see the guilt written on his face. Written in beautiful, calligraphic lettering, as though I had put it there myself.

chapter 21

Love is like a snowmobile flying over the frozen tundra that suddenly flips, pinning you underneath. At night the ice weasels come.

—Matt Groening

What are you doing?" I whispered, my voice small in the falling snow.

"I should think it was obvious."

"It wasn't supposed to be you," I said, pressing my palms into my eyes, trying to blot out the picture in my mind.

"Well, it's nice to see you again, too. How have you been?" Brian said, grinning widely.

"Not very well. It appears someone has been playing games with me. It's funny; you'd think I'd be used to that by now." I put the key in the lock and went through the door, shoving it closed behind me. Brian's hand appeared in the doorway, wedged in the door just before it slammed shut.

"Come on, Riley, hear me out."

"You've got nothing to say that I want to hear," I said, trying to sound detached and uninterested.

"Really? Because you didn't seem to mind listening when I was your mystery admirer," he said smugly.

I could feel my anger reaching critical mass. "This is the absolute lowest thing you're ever done. After everything else, why couldn't you just leave me alone? How could you trick me like this?"

"I knew you'd never listen to me, and I wanted to show you how much I cared. How much I still care."

I stared at him in disbelief. "Isn't your wife wondering where you are?"

He looked puzzled. "My wife?"

"Yes, I remember her well. We only met once, but her cakes were amazing. Of course, she didn't make quite the lasting impression on me that she did you, but I assume everything worked out in the end. I can't recall her name. What was it—Dixie? Trixie? Let's just refer to her as 'my timely replacement.'"

"It was Lisa. And we broke up."

"Couldn't cross the finish line with her either, huh? Is she still working in the same bakery? I'd like to send her a card, congratulating her on her escape."

"I couldn't marry her because I was still in love with you."

I shook my head, a short, humorless laugh escaping my lips. "I must have heard you wrong."

"If you give me a chance, I'll explain everything, but you have to let me finish and promise not to interrupt."

I sat down on the couch and folded my arms. "Go ahead. I can't wait to see you try to put a positive spin on this story."

Brian sat down on the chair across from me and took a deep breath. "We used to have a good time together, right? Whatever else you might remember about me, we had a lot of fun. Everything was fine before you started hinting about us getting married."

"I was *not* hinting!" I exploded, jumping up off the couch.

"Calm down! Just listen to the whole story before you come to any judgments, okay?"

I settled back onto the couch. I said that I would hear him out, but I was determined not to agree with him.

"I started having these terrible panic attacks. After I'd drop you off at your house at night, I'd go home to bed, and it felt as if the walls were closing in on me. It was all so final."

"Then why did you ask me to marry you?" I asked through gritted teeth.

"I knew you expected it, and it was the next logical step."

"How romantic."

"I didn't mean it like that. It's not that I didn't want to marry you—I did. After I proposed, the panic attacks were even worse. I even ended up in the ER one night. I thought I was having a heart attack. But I wanted to believe that if I could just make it through the wedding, everything would be all right. I did love you."

"Why didn't you tell me about all of this then? Maybe we could have worked it out."

"I didn't want to worry you. You had enough on your plate, with all the wedding plans."

"You didn't want to worry me, but you had no qualms about waiting until just a few weeks before the wedding to tell me you were backing out?" I asked incredulously.

"Well, something happened to make me think that I shouldn't marry you. When we went to pick a cake, I saw Lisa."

"And it was love at first sight," I finished.

"No! She was . . . the solution to my problem. At least, I thought she was." He paused, considering his words carefully. "When I was with her, everything seemed better. I wasn't nervous anymore, and I talked myself into believing that the reason I was panicking so much about our wedding was because I was marrying the wrong girl. So I called it off."

I rubbed my eyes, trying to make sense of the pile of information Brian was feeding me. "I know I'm going to regret this, but what happened then?" I asked wearily.

"Well, everything was going great for a while, just like when we started dating. I even tried a sort of experiment in my head. I would think about marrying Lisa, just to test the waters, and I felt okay about it. And then we got to the point where I knew she expected me to ask her to marry her, just like you did. So I asked her."

"And?"

"The same thing started happening again! The panic attacks, insomnia, feeling like there was this huge weight pushing down on me. It finally got so bad that I knew I didn't have any other option than to call that wedding off too. That's when I knew I had a problem."

"A problem," I repeated, unable to keep the suspicion from creeping into my voice.

"That was right around the time that I saw the poster for the ice cream fund-raiser. I was at the hospital visiting a friend, and here was this poster with your name on it. And right next to your poster was a flyer about seeking counseling for anxiety problems. I knew it was a sign. So I went to the fund-raiser, and I saw you, and something just clicked. You were more beautiful than ever, and I knew I'd made a mistake."

"I was at the fund-raiser the whole time, but I don't recall seeing you there."

"I wasn't ready to talk to you yet, and I didn't think you would exactly be overjoyed to see me either. I was sure after what happened before that you'd never give me another chance, but I started thinking, what if I were someone else? That's where I got the idea for the pennies."

"Just because you snuck around and wore a disguise doesn't make you someone else."

"Yes, but it did give me a chance to be someone likeable. You would never have accepted me as myself, but you might have more patience with a charming stranger."

I shook my head. His logic was warped, but it contained a certain amount of truth. "And you actually saw a therapist?"

"Yes. We talked about my panic attacks, and I told her about these unresolved feelings I had for you. I've been working through my commitment issues. My therapist thinks that they might stem from my own parents getting divorced, and how I can't trust myself to succeed where they failed."

I felt like I was inside a snow globe that had just been violently shaken, and when the snow settled, nothing was the same. My head was spinning; in my wildest dreams, I never would have pegged Brian as the Penny Guy.

"Riley, are you listening? I've been trying to show you how much I still love you. I want you back."

"This is a lot, Brian. I'm glad that you're getting your life sorted out, but what do you expect me to do about it?"

"Couldn't we give it another try?"

"I've been seeing someone else," I said, finally finding my voice.

"Paul?" he said casually. The sound of Brian actually saying Paul's name jarred me back to the present.

"How do you know his name?"

"I saw you two at the restaurant, the night I left the pennies. And I met him at the carnival."

"What do you mean, you met him?"

"Remember the clown suit? I chatted with him while I was making him a spider balloon animal, which I'm guessing was for you. He's not the guy I pictured you with, but at least he has a sense of humor."

"We're getting close," I said defensively. "At least I can trust him."

"Is that why you were wandering around outside in the snow at night, crying, because you're so blissfully happy together?"

I walked to the door and opened it. "I think you should go now."

"Just promise me you'll think about it. We were happy before I screwed it up, but I think I'm better now. All I'm asking for is a second chance." He slipped out the door and into the snowy evening.

For so long after he called off the wedding, all I wanted was another chance, and here it was. But the idea that Brian was the one leaving me the poems, the idea that I'd been building my hopes on yet another deception, decimated me.

I took the wreath off the door, not wanting to read the note but knowing I would anyway. I unfolded it, amazed how cynical I was about it. Now that I knew it was Brian, the excitement was pretty much gone. There was a time that he was all I ever wanted, and we probably would have been happy together, at least until the next pretty face crossed his path. But no matter how incredible the penny gesture was, I didn't know if I could ever trust him again. The note read:

Love takes off masks that we fear we cannot live without and know we cannot live within.
—James Baldwin

I took the note and added it to all the ones from the fridge.
I wasn't sure how I felt about them now, so I took them all down
and stuffed them into a drawer. My head felt foggy, and I decided
that I might as well just go to bed. I was too confused to make any
serious decisions tonight, and I had to get up and go to work in the
morning. As I dragged myself into my bed, I thought how easy it
would be if there was some sign that pointed me in one direction
or the other. Maybe everything would be clearer tomorrow.

. . . .

"So, you'll never guess what happened to me last night," I said,
taking the tin foil off of my snack bar lunch plate. Lauren showed
up at the office to show me which flowers she'd chosen for the
wedding and take me to lunch, but I was too busy to leave. So
we settled for grabbing something quick in the snack bar. I was
having the egg salad sandwich.

"Shock me," Lauren said, wrinkling up her nose as she got a
distinct whiff of my sandwich. "I always thought egg salad was the
sort of lunch that little old ladies ate," she commented.

"I like egg salad, and this isn't exactly a gourmet restaurant.
There isn't a whole lot you can do to screw it up. I like to stick with
something safe. And the nice thing is, it's the same every time I
order it. No matter what catastrophe is happening in my life, I
know that I will always get egg salad on white, sliced on the diago-
nal, with one tomato slice, a wilted pickle spear, a pile of shredded
lettuce, and four olives. I don't really care for olives, but I think I
would miss them if they weren't there."

"You've obviously put way too much thought into this," she
said, taking a bite of her grilled cheese. "So, what happened to you
last night?"

"I caught . . . the Penny Guy," I said dramatically.

Her mouth dropped open. "No. Way."

I took a bite of my sandwich and chewed it slowly and deliber-
ately, determined to drag it out as long as possible.

"Well?"

"Well, what?"

"Come on, Riley, don't make me beg. Who is he? Do you know
him? Do I know him?"

"Yes and yes."

A triumphant look appeared on her face. "I knew it. I knew it
was Paul; I just had a feeling. Didn't I tell you it was Paul?"

"It wasn't Paul," I said sadly.

"Oh. Well, if it's not Paul, and it's someone I know, then who
is it?"

"You'll never guess, so I'm just going to come right out with
it," I said, sighing loudly.

"You don't look very pleased about it."

"Well, I wouldn't be, would I? It's Brian."

She froze mid-bite. "Your Brian?" she whispered, as if saying
his name out loud would cause him to materialize on the spot.

"I'm not sure he ever really was 'my Brian,' but yes."

"That is so bizarre. You know, I was sitting in traffic the other
night, and I swear I saw him stumbling out of a club downtown."

"The last time I saw him was in the grocery store," I said
matter-of-factly.

"What? When? You never told me that."

"It was about a year ago. Guess what was in his cart?"

"Tell me."

"Energy drinks, meal replacement bars, and several economy-
sized bottles of prune juice. I'm hoping he was picking up the
prune juice for an aging grandparent."

Lauren could hardly breathe, she was laughing so hard. "What
did you say to him?"

"Luckily, I saw him before he saw me, so I had just enough time
to crouch behind a display of canned peas and corn," I mused.

"You did not!"

"I got some pretty strange looks, but at least I didn't have to
talk to him."

"I've got some things I wouldn't mind saying to him, given the opportunity," Lauren said, glaring threateningly.

"Why didn't you yell at him through the car window?" I said, grinning.

"I wasn't one hundred percent sure it was him. I can't believe I forgot to tell you. It completely slipped my mind."

"When was that?"

"Maybe a week ago?" she guessed.

I wrinkled up my face in confusion. "That's very odd. I mean, he was never much of a party guy, and he certainly wasn't a drinker. It couldn't have been him."

"Then he has a twin out there walking around. But I still don't get it. Isn't he with the cake girl now?"

"Apparently not. He said he didn't marry her because he was still madly in love with me. If that's not the definition of ironic, I don't know what is. I guess he only wants what he can't have."

Lauren shook her head in amazement. "What a jerk. I wish I could have been there when you told him to take a hike. How does it feel to finally have the last laugh?"

I didn't say anything, busying myself making a design with the superfluous olives.

"Riley, I know you're not thinking about getting back together with Brian. What about Paul?"

"Well, Paul may no longer be an option." I told her about Paul's unfortunate discovery and hasty retreat.

"He didn't say he didn't want to be with you; he just said he wanted you to make a choice. And let me tell you, this one is a no-brainer. I can't think of one good reason for you to pick Brian over Paul."

"Maybe he's changed. He said he even saw a therapist."

"He hasn't changed. He put on this elaborate show to make you fall in love with him again. But that's all it is—a show. I remember when he left you, two weeks before your wedding. How could you ever forgive him for that? Why are you defending Brian, anyway?"

"I don't know. It's just that, when Paul found the notes, he was out the door before I even had a chance to explain. It's like he was waiting for a reason to go."

"That's nonsense. Besides, he has no clue who the Penny Guy really is. If he had any idea that your secret admirer was really your ex, he'd be here now, defending his turf."

"I'm not sure I like being someone's turf," I grumbled.

"I think Paul was just being noble by giving you space to make your decision. I'd choose him over Brian any day."

"Everything was going so well a few days ago. Now, look at it."

"So, what are you going to do? You can't have it both ways."

"I don't know. When Brian and I were happy, it was the best time of my life," I said wistfully, taking a bite of my dessert, a pumpkin-shaped sugar cookie with thick frosting and sprinkles. Usually I got so excited about Halloween, but this year I'd hardly thought about it. I couldn't believe it was tomorrow. "Look how hard he's been trying. Maybe I should give him the benefit of the doubt."

"You were happy, but there were times when you wanted to punch him. When someone is gone, it's easy to only remember the good things, because you miss them. I'm just the impartial observer, so let me remind you that it wasn't all sunshine and roses. Brian is your past now. Paul loves you. I'm sure he does."

"He told me, last night, before he found the notes and every-thing went to crap."

Lauren shoved her plate away, throwing her arms in the air. "Then why are we even having this discussion?"

. . . .

I hurried back into the office, fully expecting a scolding for being gone so long at lunch. My worst suspicions were confirmed by Andrea's unexpected presence.

"I'm sorry I took so long. The line at the snack bar was huge," I said, sliding into my seat and hoping to sink through the floor.

"Don't worry about it. There's someone here to see you," Andrea said, smiling. Krista stepped out from behind the corner, holding a huge check drawn on stiff paper. I felt like I'd just won Publishers Clearinghouse.

"I thought you'd want to be the first to see this, Riley. The total amount raised by the carnival . . . $12,592.16! Congratulations!"

The nurses all cheered, and Andrea patted me on the back.

I was stunned. "Did you say twelve? Twelve thousand dollars? Are you sure? I can't believe it's that much money," I stammered.

Krista laughed. "We're sure. We counted it very carefully."

"Wow. I don't know what to say. Thank you for all your help, everybody. I never could have done it without you guys," I said, blinking back the tears that were threatening to spill over.

"And while Krista's here, I have an announcement to make," Andrea piped up. "I have just been notified that Riley is going to be Landmark Hospital's Employee of the Month for November. We are very proud to have you as a part of our team, Riley."

. . . .

"What a day. I'd say we should get ice cream to celebrate, but I imagine you'll be giving up ice cream, Riley," Kate said, looking for her horoscope in the newspaper. Kate had to read her horoscope every day, and any of ours that she thought were particularly relevant.

"Why would I do a silly thing like give up ice cream?"

"Well, you'll have to stop eating ice cream so you can fit into your wedding dress."

"My wedding dress?" I choked. "What do you know that I don't?"

"I just figured that you and Paul would be getting engaged shortly. He's so cute, and he seems smart enough not to let you get away. Look, even your horoscope says that you will soon take an unexpected trip," she said confidently.

"So?"

"Well, that obviously means your honeymoon."

"Kate, that could just as easily mean I'm going to trip and fall in the parking lot, although I am quite clumsy, so it wouldn't exactly be unexpected."

She giggled. "Whatever. I think that you and Paul are destined to be together."

"What does your horoscope say?" I asked, trying to steer her off the topic.

"It says, 'Today is not a good day for gambling,' but it still lists my lucky numbers." She twisted a blonde lock of hair around her finger thoughtfully. "I'm not really sure how to take that."

"Well, unless you're about to hop on a plane to Las Vegas, I wouldn't be too worried about it."

"So, what do you think—ice cream or no ice cream? That unexpected trip might come sooner than you think," she cautioned.

I didn't have the energy to explain to one more person what happened between Paul and me, and why I was fairly certain there would be no wedding bells for us any time in the near future. Everyone would know soon enough.

"I've got plenty of time to starve myself later. What's your poison?"

chapter 22

How bitter a thing it is to look into happiness through
another man's eyes.

—William Shakespeare, *As You Like It*

After work, I walked down to the string of locking boxes
in the parking lot to pick up my mail, and who should
be there but Paul. It was like the universe really relished
playing the same bad joke on me, over and over again. I wasn't
mentally prepared to see him yet, and I considered fleeing at top
speed in the other direction, but I was pretty sure he'd already
spotted me. I still hadn't called him, and he was certainly keeping
his distance. Part of me hoped Lauren was right, that he was just
being a gentleman. But I had this nagging feeling that he didn't
think I was *the one*. He just gave up too easily. Who knows, maybe
he was even relieved.

"Hey," he said, smiling that smile that made my stomach
twist.

His hair was a little shorter. He must have just gotten it cut,
and it looked really good. There was one errant hair sticking up,
and I fought the urge to smooth it down.

"Hey, yourself."

"How's everything going?"

"Pretty good. I just found out the carnival brought in over
$12,000."

"That's amazing. You deserve it, after all the work you put in," he said sincerely.

There was a deep pause, and I didn't know what to say next, so I shuffled through my mail to fill the silence.

"Anything new and exciting in your life?" he asked, looking cautiously into my eyes.

"Actually, I unmasked the Penny Guy," I said, watching him closely and trying to gauge his reaction.

"Really? Anyone I know?"

"I don't think so, although I'm told you did meet him at the carnival."

His face was blank.

"The clown you got the balloon animal from. It turns out that he was my fiancé, Brian. Well, ex-fiancé."

Paul's face was pained. He stared at the ground, his fists clenched until his knuckles turned white. "So, your ex was your secret admirer—how convenient."

"Paul, I swear I never knew until last night."

"I believe you." He smiled briefly, but there was no joy in it. "I never knew you were engaged before. I guess there were a lot of things I didn't know about you."

"It was a long time ago."

"What happened?"

"He changed his mind."

"I find that hard to believe," he said quietly. As quickly as I noticed the sadness in his eyes, it was gone, replaced by a silent, cold acceptance. "So, I guess you'll be getting back together."

"Why do you say that?"

"Well, you almost married this guy once, and he's certainly been doing his best to get you back." He paused, still studying his shoes. "Are you still in love with him?"

"Paul . . . "

"No, I understand. I'm happy for you. It will be quite a story for you to tell your children. Very romantic," he said bitterly.

I didn't know what to say. Paul was pushing me away, just like he had before. I wasn't sure if it was because of lack of interest or his injured pride. Everything was happening too fast. I needed time to think.

He hesitated, stepping closer and putting his arms around me, squeezing me tightly. I could feel the muscles in his back shaking, and I hugged him back, wishing I could stand there locked in his arms forever.

"He's a lucky guy, Riley. I hope he makes you happy." He pulled away suddenly, walking quickly in the other direction.

"Paul, wait!" I called after him. But he just kept walking, and he didn't look back. So, without giving me a chance to explain, Paul walked out of my life, making my choice for me. I went back into my apartment and tried his number three times, but there was no answer.

. . . .

After two days of soul searching and leaving numerous messages on Paul's answering machine, my phone finally rang. I picked it up eagerly.

"Hello?"

"Have you considered my offer?" a voice asked casually.

"Brian," I said dully, unable to keep the disappointment from my voice.

"Who were you expecting?" he said arrogantly.

"Never mind. What do you want?"

"I want to take you out to dinner tonight. Don't say no."

I hesitated.

"Come on, you might even enjoy yourself. What have you got to lose?"

At this point, what did I have to lose? A tiny voice in my head kept telling me that if I didn't at least give Brian a chance, I would always wonder what might have been.

"All right, you're on."

"Really?"

"One date. We'll see what happens after that."

"I'll be there at 7:00," he promised.

. . . .

7:35. Still no Brian. I hadn't really expected much, but this was a poor start, even for him. I sat on the couch in front of the television, flipping through the channels irritably. I'd give him ten more minutes. After that, I wasn't answering the door, whether he showed up or not.

I heard a car pull up outside, followed by a loud rapping at my door. I opened it to discover an out-of-breath Brian, looking very sharp in a dark blue button-down shirt with a tie and slacks. He was huffing and puffing and appeared to be hiding something behind his back.

"Sorry I'm late, but the line was terrible," he said in between gasps.

"What line?" I asked, trying to hold on to what little patience I had left.

"The line for these," he said, instantly in control. He whipped his hand around from its hiding place behind his back, revealing a huge bunch of red roses, which he held out to me confidently. "I thought you might forgive me, when I explained the circumstances."

"Forgive you for being late or calling off the wedding?"

"Hopefully, both," he said, giving me his most charming grin.

. . . .

We made the requisite small talk in the car, getting the abbreviated version of what had happened in our lives since we parted. I was taken aback when he pulled up to Madeline's.

"I had no idea you planned to take me here. I'm afraid I'm a little underdressed."

"You look fine; don't worry about it. Have you ever been here?"

"No," I admitted. "Lauren and I always joked that when we won the lottery, we just might be able to afford to try it. But she made it here before I did. Her fiancé proposed to her here, the first time."

"What do you mean, 'the first time'?"

"It's a long, complicated story."

"How is Lauren, by the way?"

"She's fine. She said she thought she saw you coming out of a club the other night," I said, laughing.

He shook his head. "It couldn't have been me."

"Of course not," I said, trying not to show my relief.

He laughed. "I haven't been to a club in a month."

By now I'm sure my eyes were bulging out of my head, but he hardly seemed to notice. I had forgotten that Brian did that. He was always saying shocking things just see what my reaction would be, and I never could tell whether he was serious or not.

"I bet she warned you about going out with me again. She never did like me very much."

A small red flag went up in my head, but I dismissed it. I was determined to be fair, and I wasn't going to dismiss Brian just because he didn't get along with my best friend. Besides, he was right—Lauren had never liked him.

Madeline's was small and intimate, the lighting dimmed just enough to suggest seduction, but still bright enough to showcase the lavish decorating. The maitre d' showed us to a table by the window, looking out onto an immaculately kept flower garden. He opened the menus and handed them to us carefully, as if they were made of porcelain. He also handed Brian the wine list, which Brian carefully considered.

"We'll try this," he said finally, pointing. "I always say there's nothing like a nice bottle of red."

"An excellent choice, sir," the waiter said knowingly, taking the wine list and disappearing.

"Are you kidding?" I hissed.

"What?" he said innocently.

"You don't drink, and I don't drink. So unless you're planning on treating the waiter, what was all that about?"

Brian shook his head and chuckled, like he was humoring a child. "Riley, there's nothing wrong with a little drink every now and then, especially when you're celebrating."

"And what are we celebrating, exactly?"

"Our reconciliation, of course."

The waiter reappeared with the bottle Brian chose, and Brian made a big show of swirling it around in the glass and tasting it. He gave the waiter a discerning nod, and the waiter filled his glass. When he came around to my side of the table, I put my hand over the top of my glass before he got any ideas.

"I'll just have water, thank you," I said politely.

Brian took a sip from his glass. "You don't know what you're missing. You should loosen up a little."

"When did you start drinking?"

"After we broke up, I discovered there was a whole world of things out there, just waiting to be explored."

"It probably was you outside the club, wasn't it?"

"Is it really important?'

The red flag was back, but bigger now. I drank more water and tried to calm down. Plenty of people are social drinkers. Just because it went against what I believed in didn't mean Brian should refrain for my sake . . . right? I focused on my menu instead, trying to wade through the fancy descriptions and find something I could eat. When the waiter returned, he rattled off the list of specials in a practiced tone and asked if we had any questions.

"Do you have anything with chicken?" I asked.

"We don't currently have a chicken item in our repertoire. However, we do have a lovely roast duckling with raspberry sauce."

"Duckling? You think I'm going to eat a duckling? That's so sad. I might as well eat a kitten," I said indignantly.

"How is duckling any more disturbing than chicken?" he asked dryly.

"I can't eat the chicken now either," I said, fanning myself with the menu. It suddenly seemed very hot in the room.

"We also have a veal dish that's very popular right now. It's served with rosemary potatoes in a garlic white wine glaze. And the lamb is very good—you won't be disappointed."

"What's the matter with you people? Don't you serve anything besides baby animals?"

"Riley! Just choose something!" Brian snapped, his face turning red.

I turned to the waiter. "I'm sorry. What do you serve for vegetarians?"

"We don't get many vegetarians here at Madeline's."

"But if a vegetarian showed up, what would you feed them?" I prodded.

"We have some nice lettuce in the kitchen."

"Great—I'll have the lettuce," I said, handing him the menu.

"It is baby lettuce," he said, his gruff exterior betrayed by the twinkle in his eye. "Will that be a problem?"

"For the lettuce, I'm willing to make an exception."

"And for you, sir?"

"I'll have the filet mignon, rare."

"Excellent, sir."

"I can't believe you did that," Brian said under his breath.

"Did what?"

"Made such a production out of ordering. When did you stop eating meat, anyway?"

"I never ate meat. Don't you remember?"

"I don't remember it ever being so difficult to buy you dinner. Honestly, it's embarrassing, Riley. Everyone was looking at us."

The red flag was enormous, and it was now accompanied by a blaring warning siren. I took the napkin from my lap and placed it on the plate in front of me. "I think I'm going to call it a night, save you from any further embarrassment. Enjoy your raw cow."

I walked quickly toward the door. When I reached the lobby, Brian grabbed my arm.

"Riley, wait. This is silly."

"No, I was silly, to think there was the smallest chance that you and I could ever make it work."

"I'm sorry. I got carried away. I guess I was trying to impress you . . . " His voice trailed off, as his eyes followed a curvy brunette in a strapless evening gown.

I stepped in front of him, blocking his view. He frowned.

"*Good-bye*, Brian."

He followed me halfway down the front steps, protesting his innocence before he gave up and went back inside, no doubt in pursuit of the long-legged brunette goddess. Apparently, some things never change, no matter how much time you spend in therapy.

I took my cell phone out of my purse and dialed Lauren's number. Luckily, she picked up.

"Do you want to hear about the shortest reconciliation in history?"

"Where are you?"

"Outside Madeline's."

"Well, it sounds like you at least got a nice dinner out of it."

"Sadly, no. They're probably serving the main course right now."

"You poor thing. Just stay put, and I'll be there in a minute."

"What would I do without you?"

"Probably a lot of walking."

chapter 23

To fall in love is easy, even to remain in it is not difficult;
our human loneliness is cause enough. But it is a hard
quest worth making to find a comrade through whose
steady presence one becomes steadily the person one
desires to be.

—Anna Louise Strong

W hy don't you go see Paul?" Lauren asked out of the
blue. We were having our nails done, three days before
the wedding.

I still hadn't heard from Paul since the day I saw him at the
mailbox. Either he never went out of his apartment, or he knew
when I'd be leaving and planned his day around me. I thought for
a while maybe he'd moved, but one night I saw his truck parked
in its stall. I almost had myself talked into knocking on his door
a hundred times, but it was too embarrassing. Even though I was
pretty busy with the preparations for Lauren's wedding, I always
carried my cell phone with me, and I even got caller ID at home so
I'd know if he called while I was out. But as far as I could tell, Paul
had simply dropped off the face of the earth.

"Lauren, we've been over this," I said in a tired voice.

"I know, but it isn't good enough. You belong together, but
someone has to take the first, scary step."

"I just can't. It's humiliating. If Paul really cared, he would

have said something when I told him about Brian, instead of running away."

"Riley, this isn't a fairy tale. This is your life we're talking
about, and as gallant as it would have been for Paul to duel Brian
to the death for your honor, it wasn't really realistic. For whatever
reason, Paul backed off. What I don't understand is, why didn't
you fight for him?"

"Maybe I'm not that brave."

"Whatever. I still think you should go talk to him. You're
throwing away a really good guy because it's easier than making
the first move."

"What am I supposed to say? 'Hi Paul, remember me? I don't
know if you're still interested, but I'm free now, so, if you want,
we can just pick up where we left off.' That's pathetic. Besides, I'm
sure he's moved on by now."

She shrugged. "Well, I've done my best. The rest is up to
you."

. . . .

The night before Lauren's wedding, I sat on my couch in my
bathrobe, drowning my sorrows in a pint of dulce de leche. At
the rate I was going, I probably wouldn't fit into my bridesmaid
dress, but at this point, I found it hard to care. If it were anyone
but Lauren, I think I would have been conveniently sick at the last
minute. But she is my best friend, so I knew I had no choice but to
pull myself together, put on my happy face, and go.

I scraped the bottom of the ice cream carton, having achieved
my goal of making my stomach feel as bad as the rest of me did.
If only I could go back: I would take out a restraining order on
Brian, and Paul and I would still be happy. How could I have been
so blind?

I'd blown it. Paul was the sweetest guy I'd ever met, but I managed to chase him off. And for what—a second chance with Brian,
a twerp who found flirting as necessary to his survival as oxygen.
Anyway, that was it. Brian and I were finished—again—and I was

too ashamed to call Paul. So, I was right back where I started.

I waddled into my bedroom and crawled under the covers, hoping I would somehow be able to get through Lauren's wedding the next day without having a meltdown.

. . . .

"Riley, you look incredible!" Lauren said enviously.

"Right. I could barely squeeze into this 'incredible' dress this morning. I look like a bloated hippo. But look at you—you're the most beautiful bride I've ever seen!"

"Really? You think?" she said happily, craning her head around and trying to catch a peek at the back of the dress, which laced up tightly like a corset, accenting her thin waist. Obviously, she had no unresolved issues with the frozen dessert aisle. My own dress was a lovely deep red, long enough to reach my ankles. It was a perfect match for the red roses I would hold. The bouquet was simple but elegant, the stems bound together with a thick crimson ribbon.

"Absolutely," I said, hugging her tightly and trying not to cry. Just looking at Lauren in her white gown made my eyes go all watery, but luckily, it wouldn't look out of place. People cry at weddings all the time. My eyes were still red, and my stomach felt queasy after my ice cream binge last night. I promised myself that if I could keep it together until Lauren and Stewart rode off into the sunset, tonight I could go home and fall apart.

"Riley?"

"Yes?"

"You would be happy if you and Paul got back together, wouldn't you?"

My gut wrenched. I was in no state to be thinking about Paul right now. One false move might send me careening over the edge. "Let's not talk about me—this is your big day," I said, my tone artificially bright.

"But if he wanted you back, you'd be excited, right?" she said, going on as if she didn't even hear me.

"Where is this coming from?"

"Never mind; I'm just thinking out loud. I can't believe how good that dress looks on you. Red is definitely your color." She fiddled nervously with her veil, straightening it for the hundredth time.

"Oh, I almost forgot. I left your 'something borrowed' in the car. I'll run out and get it." I had a red shawl with tasseled fringe that matched my dress, and I threw it across my shoulders before going outside. It had snowed the night before, a light dusting of white sprinkled over the sleepy world. My breath left a frosty trail behind me before evaporating into the chilly air.

My teeth were chattering by the time I got to the car, and I hurriedly grabbed what I needed, eager to get back inside as soon as possible. I spun around to run back and dropped my car keys on the wet street. As I leaned over to pick them up, I heard a familiar voice behind me.

"Am I too late?"

My pulse quickened, and I swear my heart was beating so hard I could actually see it moving in my chest. I stood up and slowly turned around to see Paul standing behind me a few feet away, wearing a charcoal gray suit and hopeful expression. His cheeks were pink with the cold, and I wondered how long he'd been out here.

"Too late for what?" I asked quietly.

"For you to cry on my shoulder. I told you I would be here, remember? That is, if you still want me to."

I closed the gap between us, hugging Paul as tight as I could.

"Hey, easy! I'm not going anywhere," Paul croaked.

"I thought you'd given up on me," I said, my voice tight with emotion.

"I was afraid you might be here with somebody else."

I disentangled myself from Paul. "I only went out with Brian once. He convinced me that he had changed, but it turned out to be just a variation on the same old theme." I turned my face away. Suddenly, I couldn't look at him; I felt so ridiculous. I fixed my gaze instead on an ancient tree, its graceful limbs perfectly iced with white so bright it almost hurt to look at it. "I can't believe I was foolish enough to make the same mistake twice," I said quietly.

Paul gently turned my face back toward his, cupping my chin in his hands. "And I can't believe I was foolish enough to let you go. I could have saved us all this trouble by just standing my ground in the first place. If I hadn't been so stubborn, I would have told you before, when you first told me about Brian. I only wanted you to be happy, so I stepped aside, because that's what I thought you wanted. But I realized something when I talked to Lauren—sometimes you have to take a chance and stand up for the things you want, and that's what I'm doing."

"When did you talk to Lauren?" I said suspiciously.

"A few days ago."

"Did she tell you that Brian and I had split up?"

"She may have mentioned that you and Brian weren't a couple anymore, yes," he said sheepishly.

"Unbelievable! So, you didn't come here because you decided you wanted to be with me; you came because Lauren talked you into it," I said bitterly. I hitched up my dress and hurried toward the door, ready to track down the bride and pummel her until I got some answers.

"Riley, wait," Paul said, grabbing my arm. "You're not getting away that easily this time." He pulled me in and kissed me, shyly at first, then more insistently. My wrap slipped unnoticed to the ground below, resting in the snow.

Paul rubbed his thumb along my cheek, and my breath caught in my throat. "Do you think you could give me another chance?"

"Could you?" I whispered almost inaudibly.

Paul's face lit up with that impossible grin of his. "That little dress you're wearing is stunning, but it doesn't look very warm."

"I'm freezing," I admitted. I retrieved my forgotten wrap from the ground.

He took off his suit jacket and draped it across my shoulders. "Come on—let's go give your best friend away."

I laced my fingers through his. "I meant what I said about crying. I'm terrible at weddings. I hope your suit is waterproof."

"Don't worry—my pockets are full of tissues. And just so

you know, I came here today because I promised you I would, not because Lauren told me to."

"Are you sure?"

"Absolutely."

. . . .

Inside, Lauren started jumping up and down and cheering when we came in together. I gave her my sternest look.

"You're not really angry with me, are you? All I did was start things moving in the right direction."

"Well, I was pretty steamed, but I think that with some serious consideration, in time, I can find it in my heart to forgive you."

"I've already forgiven you," Paul added.

I handed her my pearl earrings. "Something borrowed, as requested."

Lauren took a deep breath. "Okay, I'm ready. Let's get this show on the road!"

. . . .

Mr. and Mrs. Watson
Mr. and Mrs. Paul Watson
Mrs. Riley Watson
Mrs. Riley Madsen-Watson
(Ugh. That sounds terrible.)
Mrs. Riley Anne Watson
Riley M. Watson

I sat cross-legged on the floor in front of my couch, doodling in a notebook while I waited for Paul to pick me up. We were going to my parents' for New Year's Eve. I warned Paul ahead of time that he'd better have at least one resolution ready; otherwise, my mother would pin him down and hassle him until he came up with something.

Paul and I were tentatively planning our wedding for early summer, even though he hadn't technically asked me yet. My sisters were already trying on dresses, thrilled over their important roles as bridesmaids. Mitch thought Paul was the coolest guy ever and was just happy to have another male around to help even the score.

Lauren was as happy as I'd ever seen her—a very vocal advocate for married life. Everyone seemed to be settled.

I finished rolling the last of the pennies from the office pig and the grocery store jars this morning. The grand total was $13,881.43. I was a little sad as I placed the final penny into its paper roll, knowing that it was over. But when I look at where it started, I can't believe how much a part of my life it became or how far it went. What began as a way of dodging any worthwhile changes in my life ended in amazing success. In my own small way, I like to think I helped change the world.

I heard the doorbell ring, and I quickly hid the notebook, knowing that Paul would tease me. I grabbed my coat and went to the door. Outside, the snowflakes were drifting down softly, but when I opened the door, there was no one there. There were candles glowing like tiny stars on the sidewalk. Rose petals dotted the ground, resting in the newly fallen snow. I followed the candles on the petal path into the parking lot, where Paul was waiting. He grinned.

"Remember how you told me to be ready with a resolution?"

"Yes?"

"I think I know what mine is." He reached into his jacket, pulling out a small, fuzzy ring box. "I want to spend every day of this coming year, and if I'm lucky, the rest of my life, with you. I love how when we go to a restaurant, you can't decide what to order. I love your dry turkey sandwiches and salty apple pies. I want to be the one to kill all of your spiders. Riley Madsen, will you marry me?" He cracked open the box, and the ring nestled inside nearly blinded me.

"Yes! Yes, I will marry you!" I squealed.

He took the ring out of the box and slid it onto my waiting finger. He scooped me up and twirled us both around until I was certain we were going to end up sprawled face down in the snow.

When he finally set me down, I shivered, and he pulled his coat around both of us, kissing my cold lips until they started to get warm.

"Come on, we're going to be late," Paul said finally, blowing out all the candles.

"By the way, I think you chose a great resolution," I said giddily.

"Just out of curiosity, what's yours?"

"Well, my mother told me last year that I should pick something simple. That way, once I saw that I could actually accomplish it, I might be ready to tackle something bigger next time."

"And?"

"I think she was right. This year, I'm thinking . . . nickels."

about the author

Aubrey Mace lives in Sandy, Utah. She attended LDS Business College and Utah State University. When she's not writing or working, she enjoys cooking, traveling, playing the cello badly, spending time with her family, and reading.